THE KILLIN

Nick Ryan

A World War 3 Technothriller Action Event

Dedication:

This book is dedicated to Ebony. Every day she inspires me to be the best I can.

-Nick.

About the Series:

The WW3 novels are a chillingly authentic collection of action-packed combat thrillers that envision a modern war where the world's superpowers battle on land, air and sea using today's military hardware.

Each title is a 50,000-word stand-alone adventure that forms part of an ever-expanding series, with several new titles published every year.

Facebook: https://www.facebook.com/NickRyanWW3
Website: https://www.worldwar3timeline.com

Other titles in the collection:

- 'Charge to Battle'
- 'Enemy in Sight'
- 'Viper Mission'
- 'Fort Suicide'
- 'The Killing Ground'

The Invasion of Poland

The crushing defeat of the Allied armies defending Warsaw sent shockwaves of despair around the western world. After six days of savage fighting, the invading Russian troops overwhelmed the beleaguered defenders and changed the history of Europe forever.

Thousands of Allied soldiers who were still fighting grimly in the outer suburbs when the Polish capital fell were cut off by the Russians and forced to surrender. Other Allied troops deserted their positions in panic and retreated on roads west and north before they could be ensnared, with the victorious Russians snapping savagely at their heels.

Some Allied units abandoned all discipline and dissolved into a fear-stricken rabble. The highways leading from Warsaw became choked with the flotsam of a vast army in retreat. Thousands died during the rout, hounded by indiscriminate Russian air strikes that streaked across the smoke-stained sky to launch wave after wave of bombing attacks. Trucks, artillery and heavy weapons were abandoned in the disarray. Dead bodies were piled high on the verges of the road and left to rot and bloat in the dusty heat. The highways became strewn with burning vehicles. The columns of fleeing refugees and defeated soldiers was a grey snaking tide of human despair and misery that stretched for miles.

Yet even though the Allied armies at Warsaw had been crushed under the steel fist of the Russian assault, some units still maintained their discipline. They were the hard men; the tough, seasoned veterans who fought with pride in the face of death to provide a rearguard so their armies might escape complete annihilation.

The elite troops stood their ground and denied the Russians at every building, every corner, and every small bomb-ravaged village until the rest of the retreating Army had escaped. They fought the enemy to a standstill, stubbornly refusing to give ground without first extracting a savage toll. They received no medals, no recognition for their sacrifice:

there was no glory to be earned during an army's ignominious retreat.

The veterans fought on because they were proud soldiers bonded together by a brotherhood that had been formed in the fires of combat.

In platoons and at squad level they kept fighting as the Russians pressed. They were ragged, haggard and exhausted. They were bleeding and battered but not beaten.

They were elite; the best god-damned warriors in the Army.

In the dark days of defeat and of humiliating retreat, they stood tall when those around them cowered and cringed, and they fought on long after others had fled... choosing death before dishonor.

> *"The rifleman fights without promise of either reward or relief. Behind every river there's another hill — and behind that hill, another river.*
> *After weeks or months in the line only a wound can offer him the comfort of safety, shelter and a bed.*
> *Those who are left to fight, fight on, evading death but knowing that with each day of evasion they have exhausted one more chance of survival. Sooner or later, unless victory comes, this chase must end on the litter or in the grave."*
>
> *General of the Army*
> *Omar N. Bradley*
> **– 'A Soldier's Story'**

PASLEK
NORTHERN POLAND

Chapter 1:

The cobblestones of the laneway were littered with more than a hundred bodies. Most were dead, but here and there a man still writhed feebly, or groaned in excruciating pain. There was nothing that could be done for them, even if there had been a will to do so – which there was not.

The bodies were Russian soldiers. They had died in the charnel house of the narrow lane attempting to charge a row of bomb-ruined buildings at the high end of the street. The Russians had paid a terrible price for their impulsiveness. The cobblestones ran red with their blood, and now the stench of death hung heavy in the air.

Lieutenant Simon McLane studied the corpses through his binoculars, shifting focus as he surveyed the slaughter. His gaze rested on an enemy soldier laying fifty feet away, crumpled in the gutter. The Russian had been one of the enemy soldiers the American Lieutenant had shot. He remembered the moment vividly, even amongst the heart-stopping panic of those frantic, furious seconds when the tide of enemy troops had burst from the shadows and come swarming along the laneway, threatening to overwhelm his Platoon. The Russian had dashed from a building halfway along the lane, firing from the hip as he charged, his teeth bared as he screamed his challenge to the smoke-stained sky.

McLane had caught the sudden movement in the corner of his eye and swung his M4 instinctively, firing three times. He had seen the Russian take a hit to his right shoulder and then a second bullet had struck the man in the torso. McLane had seen the soldier punched off balance by the impact of his bullets and then stagger. He switched aim to a fresh target and continued firing, the enemy soldier forgotten in an instant. Now, in the eerie aftermath of the savage fire fight, he saw the Russian again. He steadied the binoculars and studied the enemy soldier closely. He wore mismatched camouflage gear and had body armor strapped to his chest. His cheeks were white as chalk, and there was blood at the corner of his mouth. He had fallen on his back, his head turned. His eyes were wide open, staring sightlessly, yet the body still twitched. One of the Russian's hands fluttered weakly, as if plucking at the air.

"Want me to finish the bastard, Lieutenant?" a rifleman kneeling close to McLane noticed the trembling Russian.

"No," McLane lowered the binoculars. "Save the ammunition. He'll be dead in a few minutes anyhow."

The rifleman shrugged and scraped sweat from his face with the back of his hand. He had a swathe of filthy blood-stained bandages wrapped around his forehead from a glancing bullet wound received earlier in the day. The rifleman slumped down with his back against the crumbled stone wall and reloaded his weapon.

Platoon Sergeant, Sergeant First Class Hank Block, appeared at McLane's shoulder. He was the oldest, most experienced man in the Platoon and a veteran of the Afghanistan campaigns; a giant figure with a craggy face and a crop of close-cut hair that was greyer than it was black. He stared up at the sky for a moment, his face set and expressionless, then turned in a slow circle to consider the crumbling walls of the devastated town, the burned-out vehicles and the litter-strewn ground. He wrinkled his nose. Behind drifting columns of smoke, the sun still hung high above the horizon. He checked his watch; it was almost six pm, but there was at least two hours of daylight left.

"It's a shitty little hell hole to die in," the Sergeant regarded the piles of dead Russian soldiers whose bodies choked the laneway with scornful contempt. "I've told the men we're holding our position until nightfall."

McLane grunted. The shitty little hell hole was the town of Paslek in northern Poland, and the men were the survivors of 1st Platoon, Charlie Company, 2nd Battalion, 87th Infantry Regiment, 2nd Brigade Combat Team, 10th Mountain Division.

The Battalion of Mountaineers were the retreating Allied Army's rearguard. Filthy with grime, dripping sweat, unshaven, haggard and exhausted, the unit had been fighting non-stop for almost two weeks – first in small towns northeast of the Polish capital, and then in the outskirts of the Warsaw. They had been in retreat ever since the city had fallen, withdrawing with the beaten Army north towards Gdansk on the Baltic coast – pausing at every small village, every blind corner and every bridge to slow the vanguard of the pursuing Russian force that was swarming across the Polish countryside in headlong pursuit. The Mountaineers were elite soldiers, hardened to war and all its gruesome horror, but they were isolated; caught in a vice between the retreating Army straggling northwards and the pursuing Russians pressing them from the south.

"Reckon they'll attack again?" McLane asked. The Platoon had been defending the end of the narrow street for five hours and had so far held off three enemy attacks, each one more savage than the last.

"Yeah," Sergeant Block said.

The weary soldiers waited and used the moments of respite to gulp down blood-warm water from their CamelBaks or gnaw on MREs. A few men stretched out amongst the broken rubble and dozed fitfully. After almost a full day of frantic combat, kitted out in fifty pounds of battle rattle, Kevlar and body armor, the Platoon's survivors were exhausted and dizzy with borderline heat stroke.

They were defending the ruined remains of a row of stucco buildings at the end of a street that had been devastated by Russian air strikes two days earlier. The position was on the crest of a gentle slope in the 'old town' of Paslek. Directly in front of them lay the slaughterhouse of the narrow alley the Russians had charged into. To their right was a stretch of cratered parking lot, littered with the carcasses of burned-out and abandoned cars. The Russians were in the buildings on the far side of the open space.

It was the parking lot that worried McLane.

So far, the Platoon had fought only advance elements of the Russian Army; light infantry unsupported by artillery or heavy weapons. But that couldn't last, and once the main force of the enemy caught up to their vanguard, they would swarm across the open space under the cover of artillery and mortar fire, overwhelming the Americans with their sheer weight of numbers.

McLane wondered if the main body of the Russian Army had been held up by other elements of the Battalion, or perhaps the Allies had been able to muster enough fighter jets to launch air strikes on the advancing column, delaying the arrival of the Russians. Whatever the reason, the enemy were ominously invisible, and that made the Lieutenant swear nervously.

The Platoon seemed alone and cruelly vulnerable, yet further to their right, the rest of Charlie Company were spread out along the crest of the rise, defending similar bomb-ruined buildings that overlooked other narrow alleys amidst the historic sector of the old town.

"How are we for ammunition?" McLane asked without real curiosity. He knew the answer.

Sergeant Block was a taciturn bear-like man of few words. He wasted none of them giving his opinion. "If the Russians get their shit together, we're fucked."

McLane grunted. He was about to say something more substantial when a flicker of movement on the far side of the parking lot caught his attention. He raised the binoculars again and peered down the slope. The ground before him was uneven with dips and folds, and the road that ringed the asphalt parking area was sunken between stone retaining walls.

McLane frowned. For a moment he wasn't sure what he saw. He blinked sweat from his eyes and peered more intently. At last he understood, and with the realization came a small leap of tension.

"The Russians are on the move," he said. "They're using the concealment of the sunken road to reorientate the point of their attack. I can see men hidden along the edge of the parking lot. Spread the word. I want everyone locked and loaded."

The Platoon roused themselves under the lash of Sergeant Block's snarling voice, scattering to their positions along the length of ragged buildings. A moment later the sky seemed to fill with a swarm of maniacal whistling as Russian field artillery opened fire from somewhere to the south of the town.

"Incoming!" one of the Americans cried the unnecessary warning.

The first salvo of artillery rounds landed on the northern edge of the parking lot, blowing apart the remains of a house and collapsing the roof of a three-story building on the opposite side of the street. Roiling brown clouds of concrete dust and choking smoke blanketed the battlefield in the aftermath of the thunderous roar. The echo of the explosions rolled across the sky and a hail of splintered stone fragments rained down on the Platoon. The earth beneath Lieutenant McLane's feet shuddered. He covered his head with his hands and pressed his face to the stone wall. Two more artillery rounds exploded somewhere beyond his position, and then the guns fell abruptly silent.

The quiet after the ear-hammering percussion of the artillery was eerie; a brief interlude, ominous with menace. It lasted for just a few heartbeats – barely long enough for men to catch their breath – before the nightmare of whistling fragments and thunderclap explosions and crashing Russian artillery fire began again. Stone shards and steel shell fragments peppered the wall behind which the Americans were sheltered. Some men shivered; others mouthed silent prayers. Some men gritted their teeth to stifle the urge to scream as the torture of the unending bombardment ground the Platoon down. A rifleman crouched at the far corner of the ruined building was blown to pieces when an artillery round exploded just a few feet short of his position, engulfing him in a fireball of flames.

Another artillery round landed in the middle of the narrow laneway, and the sound in the confined space was like the crack of an almighty hammer. Walls collapsed on either side of the narrow street and a ruined building's timber rafters caught on fire. Seconds later two Russian mortar rounds exploded nearby. Columns of grey smoke rose into the sky and blended with the blanket of haze and dust that smothered the ravaged town.

Even before the roar of the twin mortar explosions had been carried away on the fitful breeze, grey darting shapes suddenly emerged from out of the distance, weaving across the broken ground on the far side of the parking lot, the figures ghostly apparitions in the drifting smoke as they came up the slope in a series of concerted rushes.

"Let the bastards get close before you fire!" Sergeant Block's voice was calm. "Make every round count."

Some of the advancing Russians pulled ahead of the rest, shouting their war cry as they dashed across the cratered parking lot. McLane guessed there were fifty or sixty enemy soldiers in the attack. One of the Russians dropped to his knee in the shadow of a burned-out car and sprayed the stone wall where the Americans were sheltered with a ragged fusillade.

"Prodvigat! Prodvigat!" a voice from within the Russian ranks bellowed. "Advance!"

The infantry repeated the cry as they ran, urging each other on towards the waiting guns of the Americans, and Lieutenant McLane had time to recognize how young the Russian soldiers appeared and how ill-fitting their uniforms were before Sergeant Block bellowed the order to open fire.

They were only a Platoon in number, but the combined firepower of the elite American Mountaineers at fifty yards was enough to shatter the attack into pieces. The enemy troops ran headlong into a maelstrom of death. Cries of sudden shock turned into dying screams of agony. One Russian clutched at his throat and fell backwards, his weapon flung from his nerveless fingers. A man at the forefront of the charging wave was hit four times; his body jerking and twitching until he fell dead to the asphalt in a crumpled bleeding heap.

Lieutenant McLane peered through the swirling smoke looking for a target. He spotted a Russian wearing a uniform with a fur lined collar who was shouting at the broken troops around him. McLane aimed his M4 and fired. The Russian seemed to flinch and then his hands clutched at his stomach. He sagged to his knees, a look of stunned disbelief on his face as bright blood spilled from between his clasping fingers.

The Americans continued to fire but the shooting became sporadic as the number of targets on the edge of the parking lot dwindled. The Russians scattered, some men looking for cover to escape the terror. Others began to fall back, cloaked by the shroud of drifting smoke. The tattered line wavered, then began to retreat, scrambling back to the safety of the sunken road.

As they fled, a shrill whistle suddenly sounded.

A second wave of Russian attackers appeared at the end of the narrow laneway and came swarming up the cobblestoned slope, using the dead bodies littering the street as cover. They moved with speed and determination. They dashed from doorway to doorway, jinking with menacing silence.

Lieutenant McLane saw an enemy soldier break from the shelter of a building and scamper across the shadowed lane towards a brick wall.

"Scully! Put that muthafucker down!" McLane identified the target.

Corporal Jane Scully was kneeling at the wall with the barrel of her M4 cradled in the notch of a broken piece of stone. She aimed and fired at the target in a single fluid movement, giving the Russian a two-finger lead and hosing the alley with a short chattering spray of automatic fire. Two bullets hit the running man in the torso from fifty yards through the drifting dust. The Russian infantryman froze mid-stride and seemed to contort in the air when the bullets struck him. He crumpled to the ground. His heels beat a tattoo on the blood-slick cobbles for a few seconds and then he went very still.

Lieutenant McLane nodded in grim satisfaction. Scully wore a sweat stained handkerchief knotted over her mouth and nose to filter the choking dust. Her brow was cut and dripping blood, her face powdered with grit. She gave a savage snarl of triumph, then ducked instinctively as a fresh barrage of Russian mortar fire began to rain down. Clumps of shattered masonry fell like hail and the air filled with the stench of cordite. The mortar fire became a relentless storm of steel and flames, and the cacophony of successive explosions hammered across the sky. The air turned heated in the crucible of fury so that each inhaled breath was an agony. Lieutenant McLane crawled to the far corner of the building. Clods of rock and dirt rained down. He gulped for a lungful of air and his mouth filled with grit. When he reached the corner, he was panting from the strain. He came cautiously up onto one knee, hugging the stone wall for shelter. There were three soldiers defending the end of the building, blasting away into the smoke with their rifles. McLane peeked over the lip of the crumbling wall and spat gravel from his mouth.

"Everyone hold fire!" he growled above the clamor. "Hold your fuckin' fire!" The unit was perilously low on ammunition.

The downpour of Russian mortar rounds dwindled then abruptly stopped, like a passing thunderstorm. In the aftermath came the shrill sound of a whistle again from somewhere in the shadows at the far end of the alley. McLane took a deep breath.

"Make every round count," he called the warning. He felt light headed from the heat. A wave of nausea washed over him. He propped his M4 on the lip of the broken wall and waited.

For five long seconds nothing happened – and then suddenly the Russians broke from cover and resumed their desperate surged forward.

The Americans opened fire.

The Russians charged along the alleyway, their heavy boots slipping on the ancient cobblestones made treacherous by blood. McLane looked for an enemy officer but the running shapes were indistinct in the smoke haze. He fired at a figure dashing towards a mound of rubble. The Russian's right forearm snapped back as if it had been tugged violently, and a cloud of pink mist tinged the air. The Russian kept running without breaking stride. McLane fired again and hit the soldier in the thigh. The man took another tottering step, his face wrenched in agony, and then he sagged to the ground, his weapon falling from his hands.

The Russians were closing, hoarse with shouting and from breathing the smoke-drenched air that writhed through the narrow alley. Two enemy soldiers burdened by the weight of a machine gun and ammunition ducked into the ruins of a smoldering building and a few seconds later opened fire, spraying the Americans with streaking tracer rounds.

"Fuck!" a rifleman near McLane ducked instinctively. He was grey faced with dust, his cheeks streaked with runnels of sweat, and his eyes sunk deep in their sockets by fatigue. He bounced up onto his knees with a grenade in his hand and threw it high into the air, then dived back down behind the wall. The grenade landed short of the Russian machine gun, exploding harmlessly, throwing up a cloud of dust and smoke.

"Jesus Christ, Mallinson, put your fuckin' shoulder into it, you pussy!" the gnarly voice of Sergeant Block growled from nearby.

In combat the Platoon Sergeant's main functions were to redistribute ammunition and supplies from the wounded and dead, and to establish a Casualty Collection Point where the injured could be treated and triaged. Block's experienced eyes had been watching the battle closely as he moved about the bomb-damaged building. He gave Private Mallinson a scornful glare and then with magnificent nonchalance rose to his feet behind the waist-high wall, ignoring the storm of enemy gunfire, and lobbed a grenade towards the Russian machine gun position. Not deigning to dignify the enemy's fire by ducking, he stood and confidently watched the grenade disappear into the distant burning building. A split-second later the walls exploded outwards, killing the two Russians at their machine gun in a fireball of smoke and flames. Block gave an unflappable nod of satisfaction then glared at Private Mallinson, his eyes flinty. "Now start shooting some fuckers, son. It's time to earn the money Uncle Sam pays you."

The Russian attack dissolved into chaos and slaughter. There was simply no room to maneuver within the confines of the alleyway. But the enemy were suicidally brave. From behind the corpses of their dead comrades they began to return fire. One of McLane's riflemen from 'B' squad was struck in the face by a Russian bullet and killed instantly. Blood and brains the color of custard dashed against the stone wall and splattered the men kneeling either side of the corpse.

But despite their heroics, the Russians continued to die in droves.

Some fell dead in spreading pools of their own blood. Others groaned in pain. A wounded infantryman rolled slowly onto his side and retched. A man laying crumpled in a doorway convulsed suddenly and sat up, his hands clasped over his split guts. He turned and glared towards the Americans, his expression contorted, his mouth sagging open.

Experience and the ebbing clamor of combat told McLane that the Russian attack was losing momentum. He screamed savage encouragement to his men.

"Kill the bastards! Finish them off!"

The Americans were well trained and disciplined; they fired in short bursts, husbanding their precious ammunition and making every round count. The nearest Russians began to break off the assault and edge backwards. McLane sensed the attack was stalling, but he couldn't afford to allow the Russians any respite. He had to drive them back along the alley. He crawled to the ruins of the building's brick chimney where one of the Platoon's M249s had been positioned. The SAW was braced on its bipod, the operator hunched behind the weapon, sighting targets. McLane seized the soldier's shoulder to get his attention. The man turned around, startled and wide eyed. His face was smeared with grime and his eyes were red-rimmed and bloodshot.

"Perez, give them everything you've got. Go cyclic on the SAW."

Perez nodded grimly and pulled the light machine gun tight into his shoulder. Firing long bursts from a machine gun wasn't tactically sound in close combat, and in normal circumstances the option wasted huge amounts of ammunition, but McLane needed firepower to break the looming impasse.

The SAW roared, spewing death down the laneway behind a shroud of white smoke. The sudden thunder drowned out every other sound on the small battlefield. In the face of the savage fusillade, the Russians finally broke and fled. Behind them they left dead comrades in the gutters, and others heaped on the blood-drenched cobblestones.

When the SAW fell silent, the sound of its snarling fury was replaced by the tortured cries of the maimed and dying.

*

"Hewington took a hit in the shoulder. He's bleeding like a stuck pig, but he'll be alright. Romano's gonna be lucky to make it. He took a round in the neck. We've done all we can but if he doesn't reach a medic…" Sergeant Block delivered the butcher's bill to McLane. In the past twenty-four hours the Platoon had lost five men.

The Lieutenant grunted. He was exhausted. He slumped down behind the shelter of the stone wall with the rest of the men. Far away in the distance he could hear the soft *'crump'* of Russian artillery fire and the echo of jet fighters streaking northwards, high overhead. Around him the Platoon were gulping down water or chewing on MREs. The air was thick with flies.

"The Russians?" McLane muttered.

"They ain't doin' shit," Sergeant Block said. The man seemed to have limitless reserves of restless energy. "But I reckon they ain't finished with us, either. They'll come again, probably sooner than later."

The Lieutenant grunted. Two men were on watch at the wall while the remainder of the Platoon rested. McLane peered up into the sky. If the Platoon could hold out until nightfall, the Lieutenant reasoned, they could escape into the dark and find a new position to defend from. The Russians would not advance after sunset. They would secure the outskirts of the town and consolidate their position.

His thoughts were interrupted by a sudden commotion, and the troops around him stirred. McLane turned his head and saw Charlie Company's Captain approaching. He came clambering through the ruins of a nearby bombed building, crouched low and moving urgently. McLane heaved himself to his feet, careful not to show himself to Russian snipers.

The two men met behind the shelter of an undamaged section of wall.

"I'm pulling the rest of the company out," Captain Dwayne Creighton wasted no time declaring his intent. "We just got word; the Russians are bringing up armor. There's a column of T-72's on the road from Warsaw and they're heading our way. They'll be here in thirty minutes. I'm withdrawing the rest of the Company towards the town's train station. From there we'll head west until we reach the highway to Gdansk. I want you to hold for fifteen minutes to cover our escape, then withdraw to our position."

"I have wounded…" McLane said.

"I'll take them with me," Captain Creighton nodded.

"And I'm low on ammunition."

"You've got all you're going to get."

McLane said nothing. He checked his watch again, then nodded his head. Fifteen minutes was an eternity in combat.

Chapter 2:

"Sergeant Block!"

"Sir?" Hank Block came and crouched beside McLane.

"The Captain is withdrawing the rest of the Company to the train station. We're to hold off the Russians for another fifteen minutes and then follow."

The Sergeant narrowed his eyes and rubbed his unshaven chin. "We're not waiting until darkness?"

"No," McLane said. "There's a report that enemy armor is heading our way. The tanks could be here within thirty minutes. Keep a couple of men on watch and call everyone else in. I want to tell them what's going on."

McLane waited until the survivors of 1st Platoon were assembled. They looked haggard, their eyes hollow with strain and fatigue. Half a dozen men were bleeding from superficial wounds. He explained their orders. The soldiers accepted the grim news with blank resigned stares.

"If the Russians come again in force, or if their armor appears before we can withdraw, we'll break up into sections and start bugging out. 'A' squad will stay with me and Sergeant Block to hold off the enemy while 'B' and 'C' squads escape," he made eye contact with the Sergeants commanding each squad to be sure they understood his instructions. "How many Javelins do we have left?"

"One CLU and two missiles," the Staff Sergeant commanding the Platoon weapons squad said. The news was a bleak shock, but McLane kept his expression impassive. "Fine. If we have to separate, leave a Javelin team attached to 'A' squad and take the rest of your unit west with the other two groups. Get to the train station and then keep heading west until you intersect the highway."

The soldiers returned to their posts. Sergeant Block remained behind. He peered over the crumbled wall towards the Russian positions on the far side of the parking lot, and then looked west. Somewhere out of sight and amongst the ruins, the rest of the Company were beginning to abandon their positions, leaving 1st Platoon isolated.

"Well, this is a god-damned recipe for disaster," Sergeant Block said simply.

McLane swore. "I know."

If the Russians mounted a concerted assault in the next fifteen minutes, the Platoon would be cut off from its escape route, surrounded and slaughtered. The Russians would swarm over them, blood-thirsty for revenge.

"What are we going to do?"

McLane thrust out his jaw and clenched his fists. "We're going to follow orders and hold for fifteen minutes," he declared grimly. "The Russians will sit and wait for their armor to arrive."

"And why would they do that, sir?" Block asked.

"Because God loves Mountaineers."

At which point the Russians attacked.

*

"They're coming!" Corporal Scully's voice was the first to shout a warning. "Hundreds of the muthafuckers!" Her eyes were bright, her face tight with tension. A ripple of movement stirred through the Platoon's ranks as men took up firing positions and peered at the swarm of enemy soldiers massing around the far end of the parking lot. They were three hundred yards away. "Let them come closer," McLane ordered his men. "Don't shoot until you can be sure of a kill."

The cratered space of the parking lot was too narrow to allow the Russians to spread out so they came up the rise in a mass of bodies, relying on overwhelming numbers to carry them through the maelstrom of American gunfire. McLane could see Russian officers waving their arms, chiding their comrades on. They came like an army of ants, separating to swerve around the burned-out cars and bomb craters then rejoining again as their boots slapped and pounded and slipped up the incline. They were screaming like berserkers to mask their terror and to give themselves courage, but they were also slowing down as they drew nearer. When they reached the gruesome tideline of dead and maimed bodies that denoted where the last Russian assault had been mercilessly flung back, the wall of infantry seemed to flinch for a moment as if anticipating a fury of automatic fire.

McLane let the enemy soldiers come on until they were across the parking lot. Here the ground leveled. A drainage ditch, a ragged strip of dead grass, and a low wire fence cordoned off the parking lot from the street in front of the buildings the Americans defended. The Russians were funneled together by the obstacles and lost all momentum. As the first of the enemy soldiers began to clamber over the waist-high wire barricade, McLane lifted his voice above the milling clamor.

"Fire!"

It was a slaughter.

The range was just thirty yards and the enemy were packed together and made frantic by their sudden exposure.

To the Russians stumbling over the fence, it seemed as though the bomb-ruined houses ahead of them suddenly filled with smoke and roaring noise. One moment the buildings had appeared abandoned and the next they were alive with a fury of hammering gunfire.

"Vpered!" the Russian officers shouted. "Forward!"

The leading enemy infantry were cut down in a murderous fury of blood and screams. The dead formed a barricade of bodies that those following were forced to clamber over. Blood drenched the grass and the Russians at the rear of the attack began to nervously shuffle backwards. The wounded cried out for help and begged their comrades not to abandon them. A man with a bullet in his guts sagged down into the drainage ditch and cried for his mother. The Russians on the edges of the milling mass began to look left and right for an escape, but there was none.

"Keep firing!" McLane urged his men, his voice hoarse. The fence the Russians were clambering over suddenly collapsed under the weight of so many men. It was the stopper in the bottle that had held them at bay. Now, suddenly unobstructed, they burst forward, screaming in terror and frenzy.

McLane saw a Russian officer on the edge of the pack waving his arms furiously and shouting at the top of his voice. He swung his M4, fired twice, and missed both times. The Russian felt the heat of the American's bullets whizzing past his face and flinched, then raised the pistol in his hand and returned fire, shooting blindly. McLane re-sighted and squeezed the trigger, hitting the Russian in the open mouth. The bullet tore a hole the size of a fist out the back of the man's head. A dozen more Russians went down, shot dead on the open street.

Corporal Scully pulled the safety clip from a grenade, clamped her thumb over the 'spoon' and yanked the firing pin. She flung the grenade into the press of Russians still milling in the parking lot and called, "Frag out!"

The grenade erupted in the midst of the nervous Russian soldiers at the rear of the assault. They had watched the front ranks of their attack brutally slaughtered and knew that soon it would be their turn to face the guns. The explosion flashed and cracked flame and metal fragments. Four soldiers were flung to the ground, screaming in agony. It was the spark that ignited the enemy's simmering panic. Already teetering on the edge of retreat, the sudden explosion in the midst of their slaughtered comrades sent a fresh wave of terror through their ranks. Two men turned and fled. Two more followed. A Russian officer at the rear of the formation tried to stop the cowards and was shot in the chest by one of his own men. The trickle turned into a torrent and soon the enemy were streaming back in retreat, running for their lives away from the suicidal horror of the American guns.

"Hold your fire!" McLane cried out and from somewhere at the far end of the building he heard Sergeant Block repeat the order. The Platoon's guns fell silent and a haunting stillness washed over the battlefield. The Americans sucked in gulps of choking smoke-filled air and surveyed the terrible bloody slaughter through numbed senses and red-rimmed eyes.

"Lieutenant, if the Russians try that suicidal shit again, we'll have to throw rocks," Sergeant Block growled and held up his M4 as evidence. "I'm out of ammo, and so are a lot of the other men."

McLane too was down to just a half magazine. "We're not going to wait and find out what the Russians do next," the Lieutenant made up his mind. He glanced at his watch. The entire battle had lasted just a few minutes. "Fuck it. We're bugging out now. Tell 'B' and 'C' squad to make a break for the train station before the enemy can reorganize."

*

The two squads moved out through the rubble, first heading north, away from the Russians, and then turning west towards the Paslek train station. McLane watched the men disappear into the ravaged landscape. Once they were clear, he turned and studied the faces of the soldiers who remained. There were eight survivors from Corporal Scully's section, a two-man Javelin team, Sergeant Block and himself; a dozen exhausted warriors against the entire Russian Army.

"We can't hold the enemy if they attack again," McLane said simply. "So as soon as they form up and advance, we're going to engage them at long range and then bug out before they can close the distance. Understand?"

Heads nodded mutely.

"Sergeant Block – make sure we are packed and prepped to clear the area on my say so."

"What about booby traps, Lieutenant?" Jane Scully asked. "Grenades with a trip wire, or a couple of Claymore mines with a time fuse?"

McLane shook his head, but before he could reply, a vaguely ominous sound in the distance caught his attention. He frowned and cocked his head to the side, all his concentration on the new noise, listening intently as it wavered on the air. He shot an alarmed glance at Sergeant Block, who had heard the same beating sound.

"Helicopter!"

The rest of the group heard the engines then, very faint and far away, the whistling whine of the thumping rotors growing louder with every second.

McLane scrambled to the end of the ruined building and pressed the binoculars to his eyes. For several seconds he saw nothing but drifting banks of black smoke. Then the helicopter emerged from behind a veil of haze and burst into clear sky. It was a Russian Mil Mi-24 Hind dappled in green and brown camouflage, flying low against the horizon and coming on fast from the south. McLane felt a shiver of dread chill his bones.

"Sergeant Block! We're getting out of here right now!"

The Platoon Sergeant started barking orders and the troops scrambled in the debris to gather their weapons and equipment. Over their shoulder, still hidden from view but closing with menacing speed, the sound of the Russian helicopter reached a clattering crescendo.

McLane did not look around. He understood the situation intuitively. The enemy, frustrated by the stubborn resistance of the Americans, had called in air support. Now all that mattered to McLane was to clear the area before the helicopter gunship reached them and opened fire.

"Sergeant Block! Get us moving, pronto!"

The small column of Mountaineers scrambled through the grey dusty rubble, clambering over broken bricks, shattered glass and fallen roof rafters, moving through the ruined buildings with urgency and desperation. The thunder of the Russian gunship filled their ears. Then the ground around them turned into a frenzied wind-whipped dust storm. The world became a grey choking turmoil as the Hind suddenly appeared from behind a row of tall brick buildings just two hundred yards to the south.

The gut-melting sound of the beast was insignificant compared to the brute ugliness of the monster, its underwing pylons bristling with rocket pods. McLane felt a physical jolt of shock at the sheer size of the grotesque, humpbacked killing machine.

The shadow of the Hind swept over the cluster of Americans and then the gunship spun and hung in the air, sixty feet above the ground.

"Down!" McLane instinctively dived for cover. He threw himself face first behind a low wall of broken bricks and flung a protective arm over his head.

The evil 12.7mm YakB Gatling gun mounted beneath the twin bulging canopies at the snout of the gunship rotated in its housing and then opened fire.

The earth around the scrambling squad of Americans suddenly erupted in a snarling howling fury. Everything within the hammering Gatling gun's path seemed to liquify and dissolve. Stone blocks shattered into hundreds of fragmented shards and the air seemed to boil as the flaming gun destroyed everything in its sight. The roar was like the maelstrom of a tornado that bludgeoned and battered and flailed until the broken ground beneath McLane seemed to shudder and heave.

As quickly as it had arrived, the Hind reared up on its tail and then banked away, disappearing to the north, the predator hunting its next target.

For thirty stunned seconds, McLane did not move. When he crawled from cover and came to his knees, he was coughing and gasping, his ears ringing and his body trembling with the aftershocks of his terror.

The scene amongst the rubble was one of utter devastation. Soldiers lay hacked and churned amidst the ruins, their bodies so savagely torn to pieces they were barely recognizable. Some of the corpses had been pulped to bloody ruin. Others had been completely obliterated; reduced to mangled clumps of steaming raw flesh.

"Oh, Christ!" McLane gasped and felt his stomach heave at the terrible slaughter.

The two-man Javelin team were both dead, as were most of 'A' squad. Slowly, like remnants of some dreadful holocaust, the handful of stunned survivors clambered from the filthy broken ruins. Scully was alive, and so was Private Mallinson. Sergeant Block emerged from a bomb crater, his face scratched and bleeding. Private Gardiner, the son of a Virginian politician, was the only other man to live through the attack. McLane surveyed the cruel devastation with welling tears in his eyes, helpless and solemn. It had been his responsibility to keep these men alive. Those soldiers were his; they had meant everything to him. His duty to their survival had made every other decision negotiable, and now he was struck by a profound sense of failure. His voice, when he spoke, quavered with loathing and emotion. "The Russians will pay for this," he choked out the words, trembling with the implicit promise of his vow.

The fight for Paslek was over. They had held off the enemy for almost a full day and won the battle – but it felt like a crushing defeat.

Now the remaining Mountaineers had to escape through the enemy's lines and rejoin the Allied Army that was somewhere to the north, retreating towards Gdansk.

In the shadows of the darkening day, the handful of forlorn soldiers began to creep west.

*

Most of the Russian troops that stormed Paslek were from the 144th Guards Motor Rifle Division, a recently reformed unit that had been shoehorned into the 20th Guards Army for the invasion of Poland. The troops were fresh from their depots and had arrived at the outskirts of Warsaw for the attack on the capital, poorly trained and ill-disciplined.

Now, with the town won and the last of the Allied resistance crushed, hundreds of men broke ranks and went on a rampage, looting and pillaging. They roamed through the narrow streets in packs, breaking down bolted doors and smashing boarded over windows. Houses were ransacked and torched. Inevitably wine cellars were discovered, and the mob drank themselves insensible. Warehouse doors were ripped open and the twilight sky turned lurid with flickering flames and rising columns of black smoke.

A sudden high-pitched woman's scream rang out through the darkening night and was greeted with a chorus of drunken cheering. Soon other women were found. Those townsfolk that had been too stubborn or too fearful to leave their homes suffered the savage consequences of their decision not to flee. They were dragged from their basements and hiding places and given over to the savagery of the soldiers that bayed like wild rabid dogs.

The Russians dragged a woman into the town's small plaza and stripped her naked. She screamed in terror, but her hysterical fear only seemed to incense the drunken crowd that ringed her. The soldiers pushed the woman from side to side, the men's eyes glittering with lust, until she staggered, sobbing. The soldiers threw the woman down on the ground, and her sobs became unholy screams.

Across the town it was the same. The Polish men were rounded up and shot. The women were raped. Some women had their throats cut, others simply sobbed and suffered until they passed out. An elderly man who tried to protect his teenage granddaughter from the soldiers was dragged into a laneway and executed.

Drunken fights broke out as the Russians squabbled over women or alcohol. Some men roamed the streets half-naked, drenched in blood and staggering. Others collapsed in the filthy narrow laneways and slept in a stupor. An officer who tried to break up a brawl was shot in the face and left for dead.

McLane led the small knot of Mountaineers north through a district of ruined buildings and eventually onto a long winding street that snaked down the reverse side of the crest, leading them in a gradual loop back west towards the heart of the occupied township. The soldiers moved quickly, clinging to the shadows, hugging stone walls and hedges, their eyes constantly moving, their breathing quick and shallow, their nerves wrung tight until they approached an intersection with three-story buildings on every corner. Many of the houses and shopfronts appeared untouched by the war.

McLane drew the handful of survivors into a patch of deep shadow. The clamor of looting and rioting had grown more raucous as they moved closer to the center of town. Beyond the silhouetted houses around them, the heart of Paslek was lit by a fiery glow.

McLane studied the intersection for several minutes. The road leading west was signposted with a small diagram of a train. There was military traffic on the road; BMP troop carriers roaming the streets. McLane swore bitterly.

"We're cut off from the train station," he kept his voice to a hoarse whisper. "The main road is crawling with APCs and probably foot patrols."

"And drunken looters looking for trouble…" Sergeant Block added.

McLane thought for a moment. He felt trapped. He regarded the closest building more carefully. It was dark, the ground floor windows were covered with boards. He studied each of the upper floor windows and detected no movement.

"We have to get off the street," he said. "We're going to hide up inside."

"For the night?" Sergeant Block's disapproval was apparent in his tone.

"For now, Sergeant," McLane's voice turned sharp. "Until we can come up with an alternative route north."

They moved out in single file and approached the front door of the building silently. The pressed themselves up against the wall with Corporal Scully furthest from the door covering the street. In house-clearing, confidence and speed were vital. Hesitation breaching the building would hand the initiative to anyone who might be on the other side of the door, waiting. The only tactical solution to the dilemma was to move swiftly and decisively from room to room, dominating the space with firepower and surprise. McLane stood fourth in line. He took two deep breaths and then tapped Corporal Scully on the shoulder. It was the 'Go!' signal.

She circled around the others in the line and kicked in the door, then pirouetted to cover the far side of the building. The rest of the men in the line charged in through the broken opening, weapons raised and full of tense energy. McLane was the last to enter the building. He stood in the shadow-struck foyer while the men searched the ground floor quickly and methodically then went up the stairs, clearing each upper floor with a minimum of fuss and noise. The building was abandoned.

*

McLane had a view looking west from the top floor windows of the house. The Russians were burning the town. The flames were well established in the shopfronts around the open-air plaza, and as he watched one building's roof suddenly collapsed in upon itself, hurling a firestorm of sparks into the sky.

He shifted focus, bringing his attention closer to the streets surrounding the house where they were hidden. The district was cloaked in darkness but the roads were filled with the slitted headlights of Russian APCs and small jeep-like UAZ four-wheel drives. On the sidewalks, groups of men roamed like vigilantes, kicking in doors and howling in drunken madness. A stutter of automatic weapons fire split the night and somewhere a woman screamed, followed by the sound of another window smashing.

"We ain't gonna last the night here, Lieutenant," Sergeant Block kept his voice to a conspiratorial whisper. "Sooner or later one of them mobs is gonna ransack these houses like they're doing to the rest of the town. And when they do…"

"I know," McLane was thinking fast, groping for a miracle solution to an impossible problem. He strode across the room and anxiously checked the windows facing east, stepping past the prone bodies of Jane Scully and Private Gardiner who were slumped on the upstairs floor, exhausted. Private Mallinson was downstairs, guarding the front door.

McLane came back across the small room and peered down at the intersection. In a nearby side street, he saw slitted headlights weaving erratically across the road. Every few seconds the vehicle would stop for a moment, then resume its swerving journey. The lights reached the intersection and paused briefly – long enough for McLane to identify the vehicle as a Russian UAZ light utility with a canvas canopy. He frowned.

"He seems to be looking for something," Sergeant Block muttered.

"Maybe he's on the Russian quartermaster's staff," McLane speculated. "He might be looking for a billet for his officers. Or he might be drunk, looking for women…"

He watched the UAZ turn down another side street. It reached the end of the road, then began re-tracing its route, travelling more slowly and stopping twice. McLane pressed his lips together, suddenly struck by a reckless idea. He let his imagination play with the risks, and then made an impulsive decision.

"Scully!"

Jane Scully came alert in an instant, M4 in her hand. She crouched beside McLane at the window. "See those headlights?"

"Sir."

"It's a kind of Russian jeep. It's going to drive to the intersection then make a turn. When it reaches the crossroads, I want you to shoot the driver. Understand?"

Scully nodded. She was the best shot in the Platoon. McLane turned to Sergeant Block. "Everyone downstairs by the front door. As soon as Scully takes her shot, we hijack the UAZ."

Sergeant Block arched a dubious eyebrow, but nodded. The room came alive with a frenzy of sudden activity. McLane swarmed down the stairs and braced himself by the front door, tensed and ready to burst out into the wild night, his heart pounding hard inside his chest.

It was literally 'do or die' for him and his small band of survivors.

Chapter 3:

The Russian UAZ reached the end of the street and paused, engine idling, as if the driver were unsure which direction to turn next. McLane watched through a ground floor window; his eyes glued to a crack between two nailed boards.

"Take the shot, Scully!" he silently prayed.

When the UAZ began to move again it rolled straight through the intersection. Suddenly a single shot rang out, the retort like the crack of a bullwhip. McLane saw the driver pitch violently sideways amidst an explosion of spattered blood.

"Go! Go! Go!"

Private Mallinson heaved the door open and the Mountaineers burst from the building and dashed across twenty yards of firelit street. Private Gardiner tripped and stumbled over something soft and heavy on the sidewalk and went sprawling to the ground. It was a Russian soldier, passed out in a drunken stupor. The Russian woke up, grumbling and stared bleary eyed in surly outrage. His army tunic was open to the naval and spattered with vomit, his chest raked with scratches. He swore bitterly. Sergeant Block doubled back and clubbed the man savagely over the head with the butt of his M4, stoving in his skull.

"Move your ass, Gardiner," the big man snarled and lifted the rifleman bodily to his feet.

McLane reached the door of the idling vehicle and pulled the dead driver out onto the street. Half the Russian's face was missing, the corpse drenched in its own blood. There was more blood splashed across the interior and windows. Sergeant Block clambered into the passenger seat. Mallinson and Gardiner scrambled into the back of the vehicle. Corporal Scully appeared from within the dark doorway, running full tilt. She flung herself into the back of the UAZ and McLane crushed his foot down on the accelerator. The vehicle leaped forward. McLane wrenched the wheel and pointed the UAZ west – straight towards the heart of Paslek.

*

The town was like an apocalyptic vision of hell, lit by leaping flames and shrouded in billowing smoke. Mounds of crumbled bricks blocked side streets and fallen power lines draped and sparked amidst the rubble. Houses had been ripped apart by artillery fire. Along the main road, bodies lay in the gutters; some dead and others drunk. Groups of howling men roamed the sidewalks brandishing weapons and flashlights.

The UAZ slowed to swerve around a group of Russian soldiers and several of the drunks scuffed their feet together and threw up sloppy salutes, believing the vehicle contained officers. McLane decelerated to a crawl, his eyes everywhere, searching for a route north. A buckled signpost marked an upcoming turnoff with an arrow, suggesting it would be a bypass road that connected with the highway to Gdansk. He swerved around the gentle bend, picking up speed. The road before them snaked through a dark built up area of factories and warehouses. The three infantrymen in the rear of the vehicle were tense, their weapons on their laps, locked and loaded. The UAZ filled with the suffocating stench of sweat and filth. In the passenger seat, Sergeant Block leaned forward as if to see through the flickering shadows and beyond the next bend in the road. His eyes were alert, his hands bunching and flexing as though he instinctively sensed some new impending danger.

McLane put the UAZ to a sharp corner and as he came out of the turn a Russian road-block swept into view at the far end of the street.

"Fuck!" he swore vehemently.

The road-block was not a haphazard obstacle. The Russians had parked an armored personnel carrier sideways across the road and there was a machine gun team behind a sandbagged emplacement on the sidewalk. An arc lamp, powered by a generator, bathed the intersection in bright light.

The guards standing post around the barricade wore the red berets and black armbands of Russia's military police.

"Unfuckingbelievable," Sergeant Block growled.

McLane eased his foot off the accelerator and the UAZ slowed as the Lieutenant's mind went into overdrive. He looked left and right, searching frantically for an escape. A side street to their left was blocked by the rubble of a collapsed building. McLane felt cold sweat trickle down his back. Two Russian sentries noticed the vehicle come around the corner and roll slowly towards them. They stepped casually out into the bright light and one held up his hand.

A hundred yards. McLane's mind went blank for a heartbeat and then his training kicked in; they could either risk running the road-block or find a turnoff and take their chances in the maze of rubble-strewn alleys.

Sergeant Block seemed to sense his indecision.

"I say we go for it," he snarled. "Run the fuckers down and let's roll the dice. Mountaineers don't go down without a fight. Hooah!"

"Hooah!" the three soldiers in the rear echoed, pumped full of adrenalin.

McLane's grip tightened on the wheel. He narrowed his eyes and thrust out his jaw in grim resolve. Through the blood-spattered grime of the windshield, he saw the two sentries tense as the vehicle suddenly began to accelerate. One of the guards reached for the weapon slung over his shoulder.

McLane studied the road-block more carefully as the UAZ picked up speed and the engine reached a screaming howl. The APC parked across the road was an ancient BTR-70; an eight-wheeled relic from the cold war. It was streaked with mud and grime. The sandbag emplacement was on the left-hand sidewalk, set back from the armored troop carrier. The sidewalk to the right of the BTR-70 was undefended. It was a narrow gap, starting to fill with alerted Russian MPs, but they were the only obstacle.

McLane steered directly for the sandbag emplacement. He saw two soldiers behind the barricade swing the barrel of a machine gun onto the approaching vehicle. McLane kept his grip tight on the wheel and crushed the gas pedal flat to the floor. The GAZ's engine howled in protest and everyone aboard the little vehicle tensed, anticipating the moment when the machine gun would open fire, knowing death was inevitable.

Private Mallinson began shouting from the back seat until his voice was a litany of unintelligible abuse.

"Come on you fuckers! Do it! Fuckin' do it, you commie cock-suckers!"

At the last possible moment, and a split-second before the Russian machine gun unleashed its deadly fury, McLane wrenched the wheel of the UAZ hard to the right and the little vehicle swerved diagonally across the road, shooting for the gap crammed with Russian military police. The machine gun's glowing tracer rounds streaked away into the night as the UAZ hurtled towards the narrow gap like an arrow shot from a bow, knocking down three Russian soldiers.

The UAZ rocked and jounced and bucked across the sidewalk, crushing the fallen bodies. McLane was pitched violently forward in the chaos, his head cracking against the windshield. There was a rending, tearing sound of metal, and then the UAZ was through the gap and swerving wildly from side to side on an open stretch of north-bound road as McLane wrestled to bring the vehicle back under control.

"Shoot the fuckers!" Sergeant Block ordered. "Keep their heads down!"

The three infantrymen in the rear of the UAZ turned and opened fire through the canvas canopy, hosing the intersection. McLane drove with his head ducked down, swerving across the empty blacktop. His chest ached; his mouth felt like it was filled with sand. He realized he had been holding his breath and the air exploded from his aching lungs with a great gush. Sergeant Block sat twisted in his seat, peering back towards the intersection. The small conical turret on the BTR-70 turned and the Russian MPs sprawled across the tarmac began to open fire.

"Hard right!" Sergeant Block cried out, and McLane heaved on the steering wheel without hesitation. The UAZ lurched to the far side of the road and jounced up onto the sidewalk.

"Hard left!"

McLane swerved again. A split-second later the building beside the vehicle disappeared in a fury of smoke and concrete dust as the 14.5mm heavy machine gun mounted in the Russian BTR-70's turret roared to life, spitting flame and lighting up the night with a hellish orange glow.

McLane had his foot jammed down on the gas pedal and the distance between the road-block and the vehicle widened quickly. Darkness draped itself around the UAZ and the enemy fire became erratic. McLane drove on until the vehicle took a sweeping embanked turn and was finally swallowed up by the night.

He let out a gasping breath. His hands were clamped like claws over the steering wheel, his uniform clung to his back, slick with sweat. In the rear of the UAZ the infantrymen gave an exhilarated cheer of relief. Only Sergeant Block seemed unaffected.

"That don't turn any of you wimps into studs. That was the easy part," he muttered a dark warning. "Now shit gets real."

*

Six miles north of Paslek the UAZ's engine sputtered, stalled, then revved again. Whether the vehicle had been damaged by Russian fire as they made their escape from the town, or whether it was running out of fuel, made little difference to McLane; he had already decided to abandon the vehicle. Ahead, looming out of the darkness on their left, appeared a dense grove of woods, silhouetted against the red glowing skyline. He slowed the UAZ and pulled onto the gravel shoulder of the road.

"We'll spend the night in the woods," he explained. "I'm not running the risk of driving headlong into an ambush –

theirs or ours – in the darkness. In the morning we'll hump west until we hit the highway."

He guided the UAZ off the embankment and into long muddy grass. The little Russian vehicle slipped and slid as the tires struggled for traction. When they reached the edge of the grove, the three riflemen jumped out of the UAZ and pushed until the vehicle was concealed inside the fringe of trees. McLane ordered the UAZ covered with undergrowth and fallen branches. By the time the work was completed the infantrymen were slathered in mud and soaking wet.

They trekked a mile further west and made camp deep in the heart of the forest. The night was pitch black. They groped like blind men until they stumbled on a small clearing where they dropped, exhausted and panting.

Taking turns on sentry duty, the beleaguered Americans slept like the dead, cold, wet and hungry, through the short night.

*

The first McLane knew of the enemy bombardment was when an artillery shell screamed through the treetops, filling the air with tumbling branches and leaves. An instant later the ground beneath his back heaved as an almighty explosion shook the earth. For a second McLane thought he was dreaming, then he became aware of a tree falling and he was jolted awake to see the rest of the survivors scrambling desperately for cover.

He clambered to his feet, his body stiff and aching. Another artillery round whistled through the trees on a tail of grey vapor and exploded a hundred yards to the north, throwing up a boiling cloud of smoke and filling the confused air with shrapnel and shredded leaves. Through the forest canopy overhead he saw the first pale light of day, tinged red by the angry glow of war.

"Mountaineers, we're moving!" he had to shout to be heard.

They went west at a jog, stumbling over tree roots and gnarled undergrowth. The morning was cold, but they were sweating under the weight of their kit. When they reached the western fringe of the woods, McLane stopped suddenly and stared in bewildered confusion. Spread out before them was a flat flood plain of open farmland that seemed to stretch all the way to the horizon. He looked, not understanding, and overcome with a sickening flush of despair.

"I can't see the highway." He reached for his binoculars, a flutter of wild panic strangling his breath. Over their heads, artillery rounds still whistled through the sky, landing somewhere further to the north.

He pressed the glasses to his eyes and saw it then; the thin ribbon of grey road that would lead them to the retreating Army and Gdansk – but it was at least a four-mile hike over flat open ground.

"Fuck!" he swore bitterly. He swung the glasses south towards Paslek, but his view of the town was blocked by the fringe of the woods. He turned in a slow sweep, studying the horizon again, finally peering north.

McLane blinked.

On the skyline, atop a gentle crest, he saw a small cluster of white-washed buildings. The ridge was being pounded by Russian artillery so his view through the drifting skeins of smoke and blooming explosions was obscured and uncertain. He handed the binoculars to Sergeant Block.

"There," he pointed. "Set back from that ridge. I think it's a village."

Sergeant Block grunted. "I see a tank…"

"One of ours?"

"Can't be sure," the Sergeant muttered. "But it's a good bet that's why the Russians are pounding the shit out of the ridge."

"It might be another rearguard unit," Private Mallinson offered his opinion with a tone of hopefulness. No one argued.

McLane took the binoculars back and studied the ridgeline for a full two minutes before abandoning his original plan for a new, more desperate one. "It's a two-mile trek to the ridge," he guessed the distance. "But we'll never make it across open ground with Russian artillery falling all around us, so we're doubling back to the road to use the drainage ditch for cover." He put down the binoculars. "Move out! We're making a dash for the village."

*

They followed the fringe of the woods, always keeping the distant ridge in sight, pausing occasionally to throw themselves into cover when a Russian artillery round landed nearby. The sun rose above the horizon, blood red behind a grey scar of smoke haze. By the time they reached the northbound road they were covered in bleeding cuts and deep scratches, their pants torn to shreds and their boots thick with mud.

The drainage ditch was six feet wide and a couple of feet deep, filled with reeds, stagnant water and cloying putrid slime. McLane waded in, crouching low. The filthy water bubbled and gurgled around his knees. The steep embankment and the bypass road they had escaped from Paslek on sheltered them from sight.

The road and the ditch ran in a straight line towards the tree-sprinkled ridge where the village crouched under a haze of black roiling smoke.

McLane set out, splashing through swarming clouds of insects. One by one the rest of the unit followed him, stooped low, weapons held ready, the tension rising as they waded into the teeth of Russian artillery fire.

McLane drove himself on relentlessly. There were no orders to give, nothing to do but reach the village safely. The tension and stress of the past twenty-four hours seemed to crouch on his shoulder like a burdensome weight. He lost all concept of time. All that seemed to matter was the next step. In the background he heard the Russian shells whistling overhead and the snarling boom as each fresh explosion shook and shuddered the earth. The air thickened with smoke until the ground beneath his feet suddenly inclined and the water-level in the ditch dropped.

At the foot of the ridge the group paused in a tight knot. The faces staring back at McLane were haggard, streaked with filth and miserable. The sun had climbed well above the horizon, leaving them exposed. A Russian artillery round landed on the far side of the road, spraying them with a hail of debris.

McLane lifted his eyes and studied the slope one final time. The incline was steep and thick with long grass. Trees were sprinkled across the ridge, some still standing, others turned to blackened smoldering stumps by the hail of Russian artillery fire. The ground was pock-marked with craters of loose earth and at the crest lay a blanket of thick grey smoke. From where they huddled the village buildings were out of sight, set back somewhere behind the shroud of swirling haze.

"We go full tilt," McLane said. "Don't stop for anything. Don't pause to take cover. Just keep running. When you get to the crest start shouting 'Americans!'. Hopefully they're our boys on the other side of that smoke and we don't wind up dead from friendly fire."

They came out of their huddle and set themselves to the challenge of the ridge. Sergeant Block gave the three young rifleman a contemptuous sneering glare. "If any of you wimps can beat me to the top, and I'll kiss your lily-white asses!"

They fanned out as they charged up the slope, their lungs burning, the breath sawing across their throats. They were physically exhausted, hungry and trembling with their own personal terrors. The grassy rise seemed to stretch on forever. They ran until their knees buckled and the muscles in their thighs burned. They ran grunting under the weight of their kit until their vision filled with stars and their uniforms were sodden with sweat. Around them Russian artillery rounds plunged out of the smoke-filled sky and the ground erupted and shook so that it seemed as though they were running into hell.

Finally, the incline eased. They scrambled over a crown of jagged rocks and on to level ground, hearts pounding, swaying on the edge of collapse. Through the smoke and flames a shattered building stood before them. It had been blown apart by a direct hit from a Russian artillery round and now stood a ruined and burned-out shell of rubble. Another house appeared on the far side of the road. It was on fire, flames leaping into the morning sky through a ragged hole in the red tile roof. McLane peered through the haze and saw the outline of a tank, parked hull-down amidst the rubble of the closest house, its long barrel pointing south towards Paslek. The steel beast was painted in camouflage and covered in concrete dust and debris. He recognized the silhouette of the tank and felt an overwhelming flood of relief. It was a British Challenger 2, and as the smoke around the village was blown clear by a gust of breeze, he saw three more of the steel beasts parked close to the skyline covering the road north from Paslek.

He sagged to his knees, gulping to fill his lungs with air. His chest heaved and his heart thumped so loud he could hear it pounding, even above the incessant hammer of Russian artillery.

The rest of the group gathered by the stern of the tank, crouched low for shelter against a flurry of steel fragments that peppered the air. McLane looked at the four haggard faces around him and felt an enormous swelling of fierce protective pride. He cleared his throat, knowing they deserved his praise. But before he could rasp the words, a new voice cut through the din of explosions, its tone imperious, the words accented and almost arrogant.

"Who the devil are you… and what the hell are you doing *here*?"

*

McLane looked up, startled. A British Lieutenant peered down at them from the turret of the Challenger 2 with an irascible expression on his face. He had pale lean features, thin sandy hair, and wore a crewman's helmet. He appeared to be about the same age as McLane, in his mid-twenties, and had a voice inflected with irritation. He climbed out through the turret and onto the back deck of the tank to make himself heard over the noise of the main engine. "Well? Who the blue blazes are you?"

"We're Americans!" McLane rasped, choking to catch his breath. "I'm Lieutenant Simon McLane. We've come from Paslek."

"There are no bloody Americans left in Paslek," the British tank officer scowled. "It's full of bloody Russians."

"I know," McLane's throat was raw. "We're 10th Mountain Division. We're the only survivors of my Platoon. We got separated from the rest of our Company when they pulled out of the town yester −"

The shouted conversation was abruptly interrupted by the whine of an incoming artillery round that exploded just fifty feet away from the tank. The Americans flattened themselves on the ground behind the steel vastness of the British Challenger and stayed immobile until the swirling dust and smoke cloud had swept over them.

When the storm of fire and fragments had passed, McLane got slowly to his feet. The British tank commander had not moved.

"Who are you?"

The British officer stiffened as if to give the moment some formal gravitas. "Lieutenant Wilfred Barnsley," he said crisply, "Cyclops Squadron, the Royal Tank Regiment, British Army"

"Are you meant to be here, Lieutenant?"

"Yes, of course," the British officer frowned. "We've been sent to slow the Russian advance."

"Just four tanks?"

As abruptly as it had begun, the flailing thunder of Russian artillery suddenly stopped and the crest of the ridge fell eerily silent. Swirling smoke and thick dust hung in the air, and the buildings around them still burned, but it seemed to McLane as though a menacing stillness had fallen over the battlefield.

The British Lieutenant gave a troubled frown. He stared up at the sullen sky and then turned to look south. "Well, that's not a good sign," he muttered ominously. "It means the Russians must be pouring out of Paslek. They'll be here in a few minutes."

He clambered down from the Challenger 2 and bounced to the ground, spritely and full of energy. He shook McLane's hand. "You're in the shit, old boy," the British officer smiled. "We all are. Any moment now the road out of Paslek is going to be bristling with enemy armor trying to take this ridge."

He pointed south, indicating the road the Americans had travelled the evening before and the dense grove of woods where they had spent a miserable hungry night. "It's our job to give the Ruskies a headache and to slow them down a bit."

"Do you know what happened to the rest of our unit – Charlie Company, 2nd Battalion, 87th Infantry Regiment, 2nd Brigade Combat Team, 10th Mountain Division?"

"Wouldn't have a bloody clue," the Englishman's buoyant good humor began to grate on McLane's nerves, "but if you're happy to find a deep hole to hide in for half an hour while we smack the Russians around, you can hitch a ride north with us. We're falling back to a god-awful little village called Nowa Pilona, or some such thing. You might learn something there."

McLane nodded his thanks. Lieutenant Barnsley re-mounted his Challenger 2. He was whistling a tune as he dropped down inside the steel beast's turret and pulled closed the commander's hatch.

McLane shook his head. Sergeant Block summed the meeting up in a few terse words. "Brits. Great fighters… but they're all fuckin' insane."

McLane turned and surveyed the ruined settlement in the eerie calm. It was a miserable clutter of houses, most of them reduced to rubble by Russian artillery strikes. At the far end of a narrow dirt road was a barn, its double doors hanging open. Closer to where they stood were a handful of cottages and a couple of stunted trees arranged around a dead-end cul-de-sac of road. McLane marched towards the closest building. It was a typical Polish stucco house of stone, enclosed by a rickety wooden paling fence. Part of the fence had been chewed away by the blast an artillery round and another explosion had torn a section of roof from the building, leaving the structure blackened and smoldering. Ten yards in front of the cottage was a massive shell crater that had torn a great hole in the road. McLane ordered the group into the crater and turned to peer south.

On the skyline he could see the distant silhouette of Paslek, shrouded beneath a scar of drifting black smoke. Closer, behind a gentle rise of fields, he saw a trail of haze, and then a knot of dark squat shapes burst from around a bend in the road. It was a column of Russian T-72 tanks. They rumbled into view and accelerated as they passed the clump of woods where the Americans had spent the night. More Russian tanks appeared in the fields west of the road, spread out in a ragged line.

"Get your heads down, and make yourselves small," McLane warned his group. He kept his binoculars focused on the approaching Russian tanks as the rest of the soldiers scrambled deeper down into the crater. "There's a shit storm coming this way and we're going to get caught right in the fucking middle of it."

Chapter 4:

The four British Challenger 2s opened fire on the column of T-72s at a range of two thousand yards. The sound of each tank firing was a loud and sudden thunderclap that seemed to echo across the sky. McLane felt the ground tremble as each tank's L30A1 120mm rifled gun erupted in a fierce dragon's breath of muzzle flash.

The first two Russian tanks at the vanguard of the enemy's armored column exploded; engulfed in fireballs and towering clouds of black smoke. The air seemed to crack apart with the wicked retort of the enemy tanks' gruesome deaths as the British APFSDS (armor-piercing fin-stabilized discarding sabot) rounds tore the hearts out of their targets.

The Russian tanks following the two lead vehicles swerved left and right to bypass the blazing carnage and fired smoke canisters to conceal their advance. The wall of swirling haze fell well short of the ridgeline, but for a moment at least, McLane's view was obscured.

He switched his attention to the Russian tanks swarming across the boggy fields to the west. There was a danger that, if the enemy tanks were unchecked, they could outflank the British position and sever their line of retreat. He counted a dozen Russian MBTs in line abreast and recognized them as more T-72s.

Enclosed in the steel cocoon of his turret, Lieutenant Wilfred Barnsley was acutely aware of the imminent danger to his Troop's flank. He dispatched two tanks west along the ridge to confront the enemy MBTs churning across the farm fields and ordered the Challenger 2 beside his own tank to open fire on the outflanking enemy vehicles.

The two tanks holding the village turned their turrets towards the new threat. Barnsley's crew were tense at their stations, awaiting the Lieutenant's orders.

Barnsley scanned the potential targets through his sights, switched to high magnification and used his thumb controller to lay his CPS (Commander's Primary Sight) aiming mark on a Russian tank on the edge of the formation.

"Fin, tank!" he called and pressed the 'Align' switch on his commander's control handle. The turret moved a few inches, aligning with the CPS aiming mark. At the same time the tank's loader thrust another APFSDS round into the open breech, then slammed it closed.

"Loaded!"

The tank's gunner checked his display in his GPS (Gunner's Primary Sight) and called out, "On!" to confirm the target had been identified.

Working with skilled and practiced efficiency, the gunner carried out the firing sequence and the Challenger 2's sophisticated fire control system worked out the ballistic solution in a fraction of a second.

"Firing!" The gunner pressed the firing switch. The gun roared and the sound inside the confines of the tank was a shuddering thunder that rocked the seventy-ton monster back on its suspension.

More than three thousand yards to the west the target T-72 suddenly seemed to tremble as it became engulfed in fire and boiling black smoke. When the flames and haze cleared, the tank was dead on its tracks, the hull scorched and holed, the crew inside slaughtered.

"Target!" the gunner declared.

"Target stop!" Barnsley acknowledged the destroyed enemy tank and began scanning for another target.

In quick succession six more Russian T-72s were destroyed by rapid accurate fire, crushing the momentum of the flank attack and fomenting panic amongst the surviving enemy MBTs. They broke off the advance behind a smoke screen and withdrew south, back towards Paslek.

The four British tanks turned their venom back on to the column of T-72s surging along the road. The nearest enemy tank was within a kilometer when Lieutenant Barnsley laid his CPS aiming mark on the target and called, "Fin, tank!"

Six seconds later the T-72 was a scorched wreck of twisted metal beneath a ball of fire and smoke, slewed broadside across the road and burning furiously. The enemy MBT exploded with an earth-shattering clamor, hurling wreckage across both lanes of the road and blocking the advance of the rest of the column. The wicked roar of the explosion carried clearly to where the American infantry were sheltering.

McLane edged himself out of the crater and stood on the crest of the ridge to peer southwards. The main column of enemy tanks had stalled in milling confusion across the road, but as he watched several T-72s plunged down the embankment and began to advance across the muddy field, still firing smoke canisters to conceal their position. The farmland to the west was barren but he could clearly see the trail the Russian MBTs had left in the soft ground, their tracks ending in a wild confusion as their headlong charge had turned into an ignominious retreat. The dead and destroyed vehicles sat forlorn and still smoldering; dark silhouettes against the smoke-drenched morning sky.

The T-72s spilling off the road fired on the move, peppering the ridge with HEAT rounds that whipped and cracked through the air. The cottage behind the Americans took a direct hit. McLane flung himself face down in the dirt and scrambled back to the shelter of the crater as broken roof tiles and shattered brickwork rained down on him.

One of the stationery T-72s on the road fired a 9M119 Svir (AT-11 Sniper) laser beam riding guided anti-tank missile. The rocket motor ignited an instant after the missile left the tank's barrel, stabilized in its flight by fins and guided from the turret of the tank by a laser beam controlled by the vehicle's gunner. The missile reached the ridge in three seconds, skimming low across the ground at subsonic speed on a feather of white smoke. Lieutenant Barnsley saw the missile as it was launched and had just a single heartbeat to shout a warning across the Troop net before the Svir missile slammed into one of the two British Challenger's that had raced west along the ridge to head off the enemy's armored flank attack. The Challenger 2 disappeared in a monstrous eruption of black oily smoke and a searing flash of fire. For a long gut-churning moment the British tank officer held his breath, until the smoke drifted away, revealing the Challenger 2's blackened and fire-scorched Chobham frontal armor intact. However, the tank's left steel track, the idler wheel and the forward two roadwheels, had all been disintegrated by the missile strike, rendering the mangled iron beast completely immobile.

The four-man British crew bailed out of the static tank, scrambling out through the hatches and scattering for cover as a hail of shrapnel from enemy HEAT rounds continued to rain down on the village. The tank's crew were slaughtered before they reached shelter, struck down by an incoming Russian round that engulfed them in a *'whoosh!'* of flame.

Lieutenant Barnsley watched on, mortified. His outrage flared and livid red spots burned on his cheeks. He cried out in aghast shock, without even realizing the anguished sound of raw pain had been torn from his lips. In a blind fury he swung his tank's CPS aiming mark onto the T-72 that had fired the Svir and the slaved turret turned in response.

"Fin, tank!" he snarled, hell-bent on savage retribution. "Take the bastard out!"

The Challenger 2 fired but missed the enemy T-72. The gunner re-layed and re-lased the enemy vehicle, then fired again. The armor-piercing round struck the T-72 broadside, blowing the turret clean off. The vehicle was consumed by a huge roaring ball of flame and chunks of twisted steel were flung a hundred feet into the air. The hull of the T-72 continued to burn fiercely through the gaping turret mount. When the smoke cleared and the billowing flames were dampened, there was fresh blood on the blacktop and the shredded minced flesh of a corpse.

For a few brief seconds an unnatural stillness fell over the battlefield. Then three of the Russian tanks approaching the slope opened fire in unison. The enemy's HEAT rounds fell on the ridge and fragments rattled the steel hull of Barnsley's tank with a sound like gravel flung against a window. Through the swirling smoke screen, he saw the silhouettes of four more enemy tanks approaching close behind the first wave and knew his position would soon be overwhelmed. The T-72s stalled on the road were stationary, but behind them, and approaching at speed, he saw a convoy of Russian trucks, each one no doubt carrying enemy infantry armed with hand-held anti-tank weapons. By themselves the threat posed by the enemy's infantry was negligible. During the 2003 invasion of Iraq a Challenger 2 tank survived fourteen close-range RPG hits and a direct hit from a MILAN anti-tank missile. But the combined threat of enemy armor and infantry working together made defending the ridge suddenly untenable. He barked a string of instructions across the Troop net and then ordered his driver to reverse. As the tank's tracks crunched through the rubble, then skidded in a tight turn, he flung open his turret hatch and blinked owlishly in the drifting smoke.

"We're moving out!" he cupped his hands to his mouth and called above the echo of another nearby explosion. "Lieutenant McLane, get your men aboard. The Russians will be on this ridge in sixty seconds."

The five American survivors scrambled from the depths of the shell crater and ran. They clambered onto the back deck of the British tank, ducking down behind the massive turret for shelter. There was little room. The soldiers piled close together atop the tank's stern deck plates, crouched directly above the vehicle's powerpack.

"If we have to engage the enemy again, your men will need to get the hell off the tank in a hurry," the British officer shouted instructions above the deafening noise of the tank's engine. "Once the turret starts turning, there will be no room for you on the back deck. If we make it through this mess alive, I'll see if I can find some ear defenders for your troops."

Lieutenant Barnsley dropped back inside the turret and ordered the Troop to reverse off the ridge, their turrets still facing the approaching Russian tanks as they fled north behind their own swirling white smoke screen.

*

On a stretch of road a few miles north of the ridge, the three surviving Challenger 2 tanks suddenly slowed and stopped, their engines still idling. The hatches of Lieutenant Barnsley's tank swung open and, one by one, the crew who fought the vehicle emerged. A moment later the driver clambered out of his hatch in the hull of the tank. The crewmen stretched aching backs and blinked in the sudden daylight. The driver fumbled in his uniform pockets for a cigarette. He strode past the stern of the tank on his way into the long grass by the side of the road and gave Lieutenant McLane a jaunty wink.

"Alright?"

McLane frowned, not understanding the question and barely discerning the words that had been delivered in a thick Welsh accent. McLane nodded mutely. The driver waded fifty yards into the long grass and took a piss.

The Americans climbed wearily down from the deck of the tank and were met by the crewmen from the other two Challengers. Several of the British tankies lit cigarettes and trekked into the field to relieve themselves. The shoulder of the road was strewn with the debris of war; abandoned clothes, discarded military kit, rotting food and broken glass. Cars, small trucks and even hand carts littered the verge. Dead cows lay scattered in the fields, their stiff bodies swollen and bloated. There were civilian corpses too – small pathetic crumpled shapes, their remains crawling with flies. The stench of death and corruption was suffocating.

The British tankies eyed the battle-weary American infantry with open curiosity. Lieutenant Barnsley drew McLane aside and the two officers went striding back along the road, their heads close together, the British officer's voice low and confidential.

"It's all been a bit of a bloody mess, I'm afraid," Lieutenant Barnsley explained as he scanned the horizon for the threat of enemy tanks or aircraft. "The Army is in a hell of a state and communications have been a nightmare. The Canadians don't know what you Yanks are doing. We've got no damned idea what the Polish are up to… so the retreat from Warsaw has turned into a first-rate shambles."

"NATO?"

"Well, they're trying to coordinate, of course," Barnsley said, "but it's like herding cats. Everyone keeps saying the Armies will reform at Gdansk, but my money is on an evacuation," the British officer's voice dropped to a whisper. "At the moment everyone's just scrambling to stay ahead of the Russians… but once we reach Gdansk, where else is there to go?"

"You said the Armies will reform?"

"That's the plan," Barnsley didn't sound convinced. "But under whose command? Until NATO gets its lines of communication sorted and a clear chain of command that can coordinate a defense, we're in danger of being utterly rogered."

"Rogered?"

"Fucked," he said bleakly.

"Where are the Russians exactly?"

Lieutenant Barnsley picked up a metal bar from the debris on the verge of the road and drew a crude map in the gravel.

"Half the Russian army is massed right behind us at Paslek and driving northwest, following our retreating Armies along the highway. But there's another flying column of enemy T-90s and APCs hurtling north on a highway fifty kilometers west of us. If that column gets ahead of the retreating Armies, our troops will be cut off from the coast and slaughtered. And if the enemy column hook east and join up with the rest of the Russian Army right behind us we could be cut off completely…"

Instinctively McLane turned and looked to the west as if he might see some tell-tale sign of the encircling Russian column. He saw nothing. The skyline was obscured by smoke and haze, but he was overcome by an unsettling apprehension, as though he could sense the enemy was on the move, somewhere beyond the horizon.

"It's a desperate race for Gdansk," the British tank commander went on. "If the Russians to the west reach the city first, the entire Allied force in northern Poland will be crushed. But if our troops reach the city and can secure a defensive perimeter, those Russians are most likely going to swung east to meet up with the Army following us – which means we'll be cut off and caught between a massive bloody rock and a very, very hard place."

"You're a ray of sunshine."

Lieutenant Barnsley blinked, and then his expression turned wicked and his eyes lit up with macabre amusement. "I was born with a dark sense of humor," he said. "I'm English. We're not happy unless we're miserable."

The two officers marched back to the parked tanks and began climbing aboard the vehicles. McLane dispersed his men with himself and Sergeant Block aboard Lieutenant Barnsley's Challenger, Scully aboard the second vehicle and riflemen Gardiner and Mallinson aboard the trail tank. Before the British MBTs began to roll north again, Lieutenant Barnsley muttered a final comment to McLane.

"We're going to push on to Nowa Pilona. Maybe we'll meet up with the rest of your Company, or perhaps there will be an organized command post there. We'll get a better idea of what the Russians are up to once we reach the village and meet up with the rear echelon of the Army."

The British tankies found ear defenders for the Americans to protect against the monstrous noise of the tank powerpacks, and the Challenger 2s trundled back onto the road and accelerated quickly, the turrets of the vehicles turned east and west to cover the flanks of their advance. The morning was turning hot, the sun a fiery red ball behind a ceiling of smoke haze. The tanks kicked up a long rooster's tail of dust in their wake.

McLane kept his eyes fixed on the western skyline. The road lead them past a handful of old brick farm houses and barns. Ten miles further north the road began to climb and twist through a thick grove of woods and for a few brief minutes they were plunged into shadowy gloom. When they emerged from the forest, the route opened into a wide area of farm fields. Along the road's edge were the remains of a French convoy of military vehicles. The trucks were Renault GBC 180 heavy cargo vehicles. Four of the big six-wheeled lorries were still burning. One truck had crashed off the road into a drainage ditch and rolled onto its side. The remains of mortar equipment and broken boxes of ammunition were scattered in the long grass. Burned and mutilated bodies lay across the blacktop. The three British tanks slowed to a crawl, moving off the road and into the fields to circumvent the devastation. McLane peered, aghast at the carnage. He saw a French soldier on his back, lying dead on the gravel shoulder of the road. Birds had taken his face away, tearing off the flesh right down to the bone. His lower body looked like it had been through a mincer. All that remained was a bloated tangle of entrails and a dark red stain of blood. The stench of death and corruption was overpowering; it caught in the back of McLane's throat like a foul taste. As the tanks rumbled past and rejoined the road, a flock of dark crows that had been pecking at the remains of the dead took to squawking, raucous flight.

"Russian air attack?" McLane guessed.

"That would be my bet," Sergeant Block's expression was dark and tinged with a shadow of concern.

McLane's eyes swept the sky. A ceiling of brown smoke hung over the land, making the effort useless, but he suspected he could hear the far away sounds of jet fighters flying overhead at high altitude. He tried to isolate the sound from the incessant snarl of the Challenger 2s huge powerpack and gave up in frustration.

"That means we're still not out of danger…"

"Yeah," Block scowled and made his own scan of the smoke-stained sky. "We could have jumped out of the frying pan and are about to land right in the fuckin' fire."

Chapter 5:

Three miles south of Nowa Pilona the British tanks were suddenly stopped in their tracks by a great human tide of refugees. They numbered in their thousands, pressed shoulder to shoulder as they tried to force their way across a bridge. Beneath the concrete crossing ran a wide irrigation ditch, fed from the Jezioro Druzno Lake that lay a few kilometers to the west. The irrigation channel was in a brown torrent of flood from recent rains, making the bridge the only passable route north to the village.

The press of miserable humanity were bedraggled and terrified. The sound from the refugees was a loud undulating wail of voices and misery. They were young and old, men, women and children, all of them dressed in filthy tattered rags. Some pushed hand carts piled high with meager belongings. Some carried the few items they owned on their back. Others hauled scuffed suitcases or held pets on leashes as they pressed and shuffled towards the concrete funnel of the bridge. Their fear and panic was palpable. They were terrified, starving and riddled with disease. Some of the infirm and elderly had been abandoned to die quietly by the side of the road. The refugees trudged past a farm truck that had broken down in the middle of the road. The rear tray of the sagging vehicle was packed with people, crammed together like cattle on their way to an abattoir. They saw the three British Challenger 2s at their rear and many of them fell to their knees weeping because they believed the tanks were Russian. Some of the refugees jumped down from the truck and ran to the steel beasts, their arms outstretched, begging for help and a ride north, their faces smeared with grime, their eyes sunken in their sockets and haunted by their terror.

The Mountaineers aboard the three tanks became instantly alert, rising to their feet and drawing their weapons to their shoulders as they barked tense warnings like cops on crowd control duty.

"Stand-the-fuck down!"

"Get back from the tank!"

McLane roared for the infantrymen to hold their fire. The sound of the refugees rose to a plaintive wail that was suddenly drowned out by the sinister snarling sound of a low-flying jet fighter, approaching from the south at subsonic speed. McLane heard the whine of the huge engines beating against the sky and turned. A dark speck hung suspended in the hazed air, flying low above the patchwork of gently undulating farm fields, and he was seized by a sudden sense of icy foreboding. The refugees heard the ominous thunder of the approaching jet. For a moment they fell into a dread-filled silence until someone in the throng recognized the ugly shape of the threat and cried out in shrill fear.

McLane clambered down off the back of the Challenger. "Su-25!" he shouted, his voice drowned out by the hysteria spreading through the refugees. "Everyone off the tanks!"

Suddenly the mass of despairing refugees became a panicked horde, brawling with each other to get across the bridge as the Russian ground attack aircraft came hunting across the sky like a killer shark amidst a shoal of fish. People screamed and those at the rear of the throng pushed and punched their way through the crammed bodies in front of them. The cries of fear and alarm grew louder, only heightening the rising terror that spread like contagion through the mass. A dog barked and snarled, then savaged the ankle of a man. A woman with a baby in her arms was pushed to the ground and fell screaming, both the mother and child trampled to death in the crush. An elderly woman clutched at her chest and sank slowly to the ground, her gasps for breath and the shrill wail of her voice ignored. A Polish priest offered a hand of help to a young boy who had become separated from his parents in the mayhem. Someone elbowed the priest in the mouth, and he slumped to the ground spitting blood and sobbing in pain. A handcart packed with old furniture overturned and was splintered underfoot.

McLane and Sergeant Block watched the mindless selfish panic and knew they were helpless to do anything. They ran to the side of the blacktop where a steel guardrail offered meager shelter from the fast-approaching Su-25.

Lieutenant Barnsley realized a Russian air attack was imminent and ordered his three tanks to disperse off the highway. The Challenger 2s plunged off the road to the east just as the Russian Su-25 'Frogfoot' opened fire on the bridge with its Gryazev-Shipunov GSh-30-2 dual barrel autocannon. The carnage the hail of machine gun fire wrecked on the defenseless horde of fleeing Polish civilians was gruesome. Dozens of men, women and children were slaughtered at the approach to the bridge, scythed down in cold-blooded murder. Some were cut to pieces and died instantly. Those less fortunate were left cruelly wounded and bled out in excruciating pain. The 'Frogfoot' swept overhead and flew on northwards, then turned and banked tightly, circling back to the dead and dying for a second attack.

The hordes of civilians crowded onto the bridge became an insane rabble. Shots were fired and punches were thrown. A young girl was kicked in the face, and an elderly man was shoved over the steel guard rail and plunged, screaming, to the ground far below. High-pitched piercing shrieks punctured the rising clamor as the Russian ground attack aircraft flashed closer.

The 'Frogfoot' gained a little altitude as the pilot made his approach and then suddenly he released four BETAB-500 SHP bombs. The munitions dropped from pylons under the Su-25s wings and fell from the sky. A moment after being released, a parachute deployed from the tail section of each bomb. The weapons stabilized into a nose-down attitude and a rocket motor activated, driving the bombs into the concrete structure of the bridge before they exploded.

The bombs exploded one second apart. One struck north of the bridge, cratering the blacktop and killing over forty Polish refugees. The remaining three bombs all struck the bridge's span and impacted with consecutive deafening roars. The five-hundred-kilogram BETAB-500 bombs were specifically designed to penetrate and destroy concrete structures such as bridges and runways. The bridge over the flooding irrigation channel split open, then seemed to heave up, hurling the stranded refugees off their feet. The support pylons fractured, and fifty feet of road broke loose and fell to the ground. The great span of the bridge snapped in two and without the center section to support the northern and southern approaches, the entire structure collapsed in a monstrous rending, tearing billow of smoke and fire and dust.

McLane and the rest of the Mountaineers could only watch on in helpless impotence as first the southern, and then the northern arms of the bridge fractured and fell. Hundreds of Polish refugees stranded on the collapsing bridge plummeted to their deaths. Their shrill, terrified screams sounded all the way to their inevitable doom. The few who didn't die in the initial horror of the collapse were killed by falling chunks of concrete and steel debris.

"What can we do?" Jane Scully was aghast.

"Nothing," McLane said severely. "We have to find another way across the river and pray that Su-25 doesn't come back."

"But there might be survivors…" Corporal Scully's expression was a plea for compassion.

McLane kept his face impassive; there was no time for the human side of his personality. The professional soldier in him shouted down his conscience's cries for solicitude. The mission was all that mattered; his only responsibility was to get his troops to safety.

He turned his back on the devastation at the bridge and looked east to where the three British Challenger 2s were hull down in the nearby fields. "Come on!" he said harshly, barking his orders. The gaping expanse of collapsed bridge was still shrouded in billowing clouds of dust. "Get to the Challengers."

. The infantrymen and Sergeant Block rose from where they had been sheltering and pushed their way across the street. Those refugees who had not died in the bridge collapse were milling like cattle, wailing with grief and shock. McLane seized one woman cruelly by the arm to snap her from her hysteria. Her gaunt face was blanched white by trauma, her eyes enormous and streaming tears, smudged with dark bruises of fatigue and grief. She gulped for breath, trembling uncontrollably. McLane spun the woman off balance and she fell against his chest. She struggled frantically to break free of his grip, but he held her easily and pressed his face close to hers.

"Is there another way across the irrigation channel?" he snarled at her. "Is there another bridge anywhere nearby?"

She seemed not to hear. Her breath rattled in her chest and her eyes became enormous. He shook her violently. "Is there another bridge nearby?" he barked the question like he was bellowing an order on the parade ground.

The woman's haunted eyes fastened on McLane's and came into focus. He saw the change in her expression, like a hypnotist's subject suddenly coming awake. She turned and pointed mutely to the west.

"A bridge?"

The woman nodded her head.

"How far?"

She said nothing.

"How far?" he growled. The sound of the Russian Su-25 had receded and become faint on the fluttering breeze. He stole a glance to the south and saw the 'Frogfoot' low on the horizon on a course for Warsaw. "How far?" he let his temper flare.

"Five kilometers... maybe six," she blurted in heavily accented English.

"What kind of a bridge is it?"

"Stone," she said.

McLane let the woman go. She stood, rooted to the spot for a moment, and then slowly sagged to her knees and began to weep, her face buried in her hands, her body bowed forward and rocking with grief. McLane left her there and sprinted for the British tanks. Lieutenant Barnsley was leaning out through the cupola of the tank's turret hatch.

"There's another bridge," McLane shouted as he ran. "Five clicks to the west."

"We've got a bigger problem," the British Lieutenant said, pointing to the eastern skyline. "There's half a dozen bloody Russian armored cars approaching."

McLane stopped and stared.

Still just vague dots several miles away and silhouetted against a low ridge, six dark box-like shapes drifted in and out of view behind a scar of brown smoke.

"Probably scouts, and probably Kurganets-25s," Lieutenant Barnsley opined.

"Problem?"

"No," the British officer said, "but it's what's behind them that bothers me. There must be more armor and more infantry trailing them."

"What do we do?"

"We fire at the bastards," Barnsley said, "and then we run like bloody hell and hope we can find this bridge of yours before the rest of the Russians catch up."

The Russian armored infantry fighting vehicles swooped down off the ridgeline and came jouncing at high speed through a ploughed field. The three Challenger 2s waited until the range was three thousand yards.

The Kurganets-25s had been designed by the Russians to succeed the BMD-4; it was a tracked vehicle that had been influenced in its appearance by western APCs such as the M2A3 Bradley and the British Warrior. Their turbo-charged diesel powerplants could push the AIFV across the ground at over a hundred kilometers an hour. They were armed with a 30mm autocannon and two Kornet ATGMs. The 9M133 Kornet missiles were a threat to Allied armor, and Barnsley had no intention of allowing the Russians the chance to return fire.

The Kurganets-25s came racing on at high-speed intent on preying on the civilians massed at the edge of the destroyed bridge. Their tracks churned up the soft ground and trailed a spray of thrown mud in their wake. They came forward carelessly, blithely unaware that three Allied tanks were crouched, ready to pounce.

"Fin APC!" Lieutenant Barnsley barked the order and the three Challenger 2s fired almost in unison.

Hull down and still unsighted by the Russians, the Challengers scored successive hits on the advancing Kurganets-25s, destroying the three leading vehicles. Eight seconds later the fourth Russian vehicle exploded in a fireball of bright flames and black oily smoke. Huge chunks of twisted burning metal were flung high into the sky. The remaining two enemy APCs veered left and right, frantically searching for cover that did not exist. The Challenger 2s hunted them like wild game, destroying the remaining two vehicles before they could retreat to safety. Pyres of black oily smoke billowed into the sky.

Barnsley flung open his commander's turret hatch and blinked in the bright daylight. "Get your men aboard, Lieutenant McLane. We're moving out – right now."

*

With the American soldiers aboard, the three Challenger 2s reversed up onto the embankment of the road and then down the opposite slope, putting the raised stretch of highway between them and the eastern skyline before they turned around and dashed westward. They followed the banks of the irrigation channel, the huge steel beasts slipping and slewing in the marsh-like ground. Lieutenant Barnsley kept his head raised through the open commander's hatch; the loader likewise in the hatch beside him. The loader had a pair of high-powered binoculars to his eyes, scanning the terrain ahead as the tanks pushed west.

The bank of the irrigation channel suddenly firmed and the a dirt trail emerged, wending its way across lush fertile farmland.

McLane cast his eyes forward, past the obstruction of the tank's turret, and saw a small decrepit stone building beneath a clump of tall trees in the distance. The windows and doors were black holes, the roof sagging and overgrown with moss and weeds. The British tanks slowed and approached cautiously. McLane and his men dismounted and ran forward in loose order, scouting the terrain. When they had cleared the area of any potential threats, McLane waved the tanks forward. Lieutenant Barnsley leaned down from his turret cupola.

"Any sign of the bridge?"

McLane shook his head. The infantry continued scouting west. Barnsley ordered the turrets of each Challenger 2 turned back towards the eastern horizon and nosed his tank in behind the cover of the old farm building. McLane was gone for fifteen fretful minutes. When he and his troops returned, they were sweating and short of breath.

"We found the bridge. It's about a mile further west," he pointed into the distance. "There's an old road and a bridge that crosses the irrigation channel. The road doesn't look like it's been used for decades, but the bridge is intact. There are a handful of farm buildings beyond those trees," he pointed again to a fringe of beech trees. "The road runs right between the buildings and continues north."

"Is the bridge passable?" Lieutenant Barnsley's expression became pinched with concern. Each Challenger 2 weighed seventy tons.

"It's solid," McLane confirmed. "And it's wide. The road must have been a main route north in the years before the highway we were on was built."

Barnsley nodded and the two remaining tanks in his Troop reversed west while his Challenger 2 remained to cover their withdrawal. He sensed movement to the east, but it was nothing more than drifting smoke. He peered into the distance, his brow furrowed in concentration and watched the drifting smudge as it moved beyond a low rise. It might have been lingering dust from the collapsed bridge – or it might have been the diesel exhaust of Russian armor closing on his position. He snapped an order over the Troop net in a tone that reflected his apprehension.

"Move your bloody arses, One-One and One-Two."

Once the two Challengers were through the fringe of beeches and out of sight, he ordered his driver to follow.

A dark, squat silhouette appeared atop the distant rise just as he moved out of cover. It was a Russian T-90 MBT, still five thousand yards to the east and well out of effective range. Two more enemy tanks crested the slope.

"Enemy armor to the east approaching fast!" Barnsley passed on the report to his other vehicle commanders. "Get your tanks across that bloody bridge."

He ordered his driver to accelerate in reverse. The Challenger 2 plowed through the fringe of trees and into yet another open farm field. To the south stretched an old disused road, the verges crumbling, the blacktop overgrown with long grass and weeds. A cluster of stone buildings were built close together on either side of the road. The houses had been long-abandoned and left for nature to reclaim. They were covered in vines and the roof tiles were cracked; the rafters filled with roosting birds.

Lieutenant Barnsley watched on anxiously as the first Challenger 2 lined up for the bridge and rolled slowly forward. The Sergeant commanding the vehicle leaned right out of his hatch atop the turret, his head moving from side to side as he checked the approach. The American infantry held their breath. The tank rumbled onto the old stone bridge, clearing the waist high parapet on either side by less than a yard. Satisfied, the Sergeant lowered his head and spoke into his headset. The tank's huge engine roared and it trundled forward.

A sudden ear-splitting whistle followed by a massive explosion sent a shockwave of alarm through the British tanks. Lieutenant Barnsley's head snapped round.

A hundred yards to the south, the ground close to the disused road erupted in a massive explosion of earth and searing fire. It was followed a few seconds later by another explosion that flattened one of the abandoned buildings sending shattered stone fragments flailing through the air and a massive column of boiling smoke into the sky. McLane and the rest of his troops flung themselves to the ground and pressed their faces into the long grass.

Lieutenant Barnsley swung round in his hatch and saw a handful of Russian T-90 tanks advancing from the south, bludgeoning their way at high speed through long grass. They had appeared from behind a stand of trees several thousand yards away, firing HEAT rounds as they closed.

"Two, get over that bridge and find cover," Barnsley snapped, then ordered his driver to advance to the shelter of the closest building from where he could hold off the Russians. He slid down inside the turret and pulled the hatch closed behind him. McLane scrambled to his feet and waved his arm. "Come on, Mountaineers. Move your fuckin' asses. We're getting over the bridge now! Go! Go! Go!"

The five soldiers went at a sprint, dodging and zig-zagging as a third Russian HEAT round landed on the far side of the irrigation channel, a hundred yards to the east.

McLane reached the northern bank and threw himself down into the reeds that grew close to the water's edge. The man-made trench was close to breaking its banks with the overflow of storm water spilling from the nearby lake. There was no cover; the ground to the north of the bridge was flat, featureless farmland that had been ploughed into long corrugated furrows. "Keep your heads down!"

Two more Russian HEAT rounds landed amidst the buildings on the southern side of the bridge. Stone slabs and brickwork fell on Barnsley's parked Challenger 2 like hail. Another building's roof caught fire, shrouding the entire area in thick smoke.

Lieutenant Barnsley held his fire. He felt no great threat from the approaching enemy tanks from the south while they were firing from long range; his real concern was being caught in a pincer between the enemy tanks closing on him and those he had seen to the east, now somewhere hidden behind the fringe of beech trees. There were eight periscopes mounted around the interior of Barnsley's cupola. He looked through the stern scope and saw the second Challenger 2 making its approach to the bridge. The first vehicle had completed the crossing and had turned back to face south, taking up a position that gave a clear sight along the old road.

"One-One, check east. One-Two, move it, man. Get across that bridge."

An incoming Russian round exploded somewhere just beyond the tank's hull, the impact so violent that the Challenger 2 rocked and swayed. Barnsley kept his eye pressed to the periscope and saw the second Troop tank finally reach the gentle crest of the stone bridge and rumble down the far side. The moment the tank was safely on the northern bank, he turned in the cupola and studied the approaching Russian tanks through his sights. The nearest T-90 was three thousand yards away. He switched to high magnification, laid his CPS aiming mark on the target and pressed the Align switch. The huge steel turret turned a few inches.

"Fin tank!"

The vehicle's crew moved with the discipline and precision that only came from long hours of relentless training.

"Loaded!"

"On!" the gunner lased the target and then barked, "Firing!"

The Challenger 2 seemed to pulse and shudder as the armor-piercing round exploded from the 120mm rifled barrel, followed by a long mushrooming flash of flame. The fireball lasted just a split second before the tank's fume extractor dissipated the flare.

The round struck the T-90 flush on the hull. The enemy tank disappeared behind black smoke and a flash of roiling orange fire. For a long moment the smoke billowed across the battlefield and then the T-90 emerged, its hull scorched and scarred, but still intact.

"Reverse!" Barnsley gave the order to his driver. "Get us across the bridge!"

The tank's hull and turret pirouetted in unison until the vehicle faced forward and the turret faced the rear. The Challenger 2 took the bridge crossing at speed, throwing caution to the wind. Barnsley ordered his gunner to fire one last time at the Russians, not even bothering to watch the fall of shot, and then reached for a hand-hold as the British tank bucked and lurched its way over the old stone crossing. The tank slammed down on the northern bank and slewed round in the mud three hundred yards north of the irrigation channel.

The Russian tanks closing from the south were two thousand yards away. To the east he could now see past the fringe of beech trees. He counted four more T-90's converging on the crossing. They were broadside to his Challenger 2s and for a split second he considered firing and then rejected the notion. The tank already had an APFSDS round in the breach. With FIN loaded already, Barnsley knew it was easier to expend the round than remove it and reload.

"Fin, bridge!"

The round blasted from the long barrel of the tank and struck the crest of the stone bridge. Barnsley didn't wait for the smoke and dust to clear.

"Load HESH!"

The loader slammed a high-explosive squash head round into the breach.

"Loaded!"

Barnsley watched on through the commander's viewing prism.

"Firing!"

The tank's huge gun roared its fury and the stone bridge exploded into a million shattered fragments. Concrete dust and slabs of stone erupted into the air and came splashing down in the raging water and across the cluster of small stone buildings. A haze of thick choking dust enveloped the crossing. Barnsley added to the billowing turmoil by ordering each tank in the Troop to fire smoke.

The Challenger 2 was equipped with five L8 smoke grenade dischargers on each side of the turret. The grenades exploded with a cough of sound, and a bloom of white swirling smoke began to spread across the battlefield.

"Rolling coal!" Barnsley said and a few seconds later the great tank's massive twelve hundred horsepower twin turbo diesel engine began to rev as diesel fuel was injected into the vehicle's exhaust manifolds. The hot exhaust gasses burned the diesel to create additional thick white smoke that poured out of the tank's stern exhaust pipes, blanketing the entire area in a billowing white wall of haze.

"Withdraw north," Barnsley spoke across the Troop net as the choking smoke blotted out the sky.

McLane saw the British tanks turning in the muddy ground. The American soldiers dashed from their cover and climbed aboard. McLane slumped down on the hard steel deck plate and felt a wave of exhausted relief wash over him. Sergeant Block punched him hard in the shoulder. "This ain't no time for patting yourself on the back, Lieutenant," the gnarly old Sergeant scowled, his face dark and thunderous as a storm cloud. "We're still a long way from Gdansk and there's a lot more killin' to be done before we reach safety."

Chapter 6:

Four miles northeast of the stone bridge the British tanks stopped at a farm on the outskirts of a deserted village. The farm house was a sprawling stone building comprising an adjoined kitchen, living area and two bedrooms, with a barn attached at the western end. The building had been constructed on a small crown of land to avoid flooding from the nearby Jezioro Druzno Lake and was accessed by a ragged path of stepping stones at the end of a muddy tire-rutted trail. The farm had been abandoned several days before: rifleman Scully found dirty dishes in the sink and food left rotting on the counter. The interior swarmed with flies. McLane waited for Lieutenant Barnsley to climb down from his tank. The two men stepped into the sudden gloom and found a wooden table in the living area.

Both men took a long moment to study and assess his companion properly for the first time since the frantic moment they had met on the ridge north of Paslek.

Physically they were in stark contrast: McLane was a tall, brawny man with a big-boned frame and a square, rugged jaw. His face was scarred across his brow, his hands the size of baseball mitts. The English tank commander was slim and elegant with a lithe physique and a long beaked nose. He was superficially handsome, with noble features. Yet for all their differences, they had the same dark gaze; the troubled eyes of men who had seen combat, who had led their men into war, and who would fight to the death to get their troops home safely. Without a word they seemed to recognize the quality in each other, and that recognition became the foundation of their trust.

Lieutenant Barnsley unfolded a tattered road map and spread it across the tabletop. It wasn't a military map – it had come from a tourist shop in Gdansk. There were advertisements around the edges of the page.

"This is where we are," Barnsley creased the paper with his thumbnail, "about ten kilometers south of Elblag. When we passed through there a couple of days ago on our way towards Paslek, the city was being evacuated."

"Do we still have troops garrisoning the city? A rearguard?"

Barnsley shrugged. "The Russians are moving too fast for us to prepare defenses. They keep hitting us before we have a chance to consolidate and coordinate. The troops I saw in Elblag were moving north towards Gdansk."

McLane leaned over the map, his brow furrowed. "It's over sixty kilometers from here to the Baltic Sea," he calculated.

"Yes."

"We'll never make it."

"Probably not," Barnsley admitted bleakly. "And if the Russians pursuing us don't catch up with us, there is a good chance the enemy Army moving north along the E75 highway will." With his finger he traced a route to the west of their position that ran north from the outskirts of Torun all the way to the coast. "The last report we had claimed there were Russian advance elements in Grudziadz."

"Christ," McLane breathed. "Should we make a mad dash for safety?"

"I rather think not," Barnsley frowned, considering the option. "Most likely we'll just blunder into trouble." He seemed to stare at a place on the wall for a moment before he finally turned and spoke again. "I think…" he assembled his thoughts as he spoke, "… that our best option is to proceed with caution. Softly, softly, catchee monkey."

"What the fuck…?"

"It's an old English proverb. It means that if we don't rush and if we avoid being hasty, we might be able to survive."

"You want to stay off the roads?"

"Yes. And stay unnoticed. It's our best chance of surviving to fight another day."

One of the British tank crew came into the farm house, stooping low beneath the lintel of the front door. He carried two China mugs in his hands. "I thought a nice cuppa might hit the spot, skip," he handed a mug with a British flag on the side to Lieutenant Barnsley. "And one for you too, sir," he offered the remaining mug to McLane. "We've run out of milk but there's three sugars in each," he said by way of an explanation.

"Very good, Thurlow," Barnsley took the steaming mug of dark tea with unfeigned appreciation. "Open up the brew box and see what we can do for the rest of our American friends, will you. And you better refill the BV. I'm not sure we'll get another chance this side of Elblag."

The tankie bobbed his head and backed out of the room. Barnsley considered the American infantry Lieutenant over the rim of his mug. "Making a cup of tea is an art form," he said. "It's something you Yanks never acquired an appreciation for. Maybe," he said delicately, "it was because you thought tea should be poured into Boston harbor, rather than a mug…"

It took a moment for McLane to recognize the witty jab. He took a sip of the sweetened tea and pulled a face. "Only you Brits would stop a war for a cup of god-damned tea."

"I honestly couldn't think of a better reason…"

The two men drank quickly. "Your men respect you," McLane offered the professional praise. "They're a well-drilled, disciplined unit. Do you push them hard?"

"They're rogues and scoundrels," Lieutenant Barnsley said with a flicker of fondness. "Jenkins? The gunner who just delivered the tea? He's Welsh, so he's officially mad. But back in England he had a contract to play football with Wrexham A.F.C. On a soccer field the man is a magician… but he turned his back on the money and the career to join the Royal Tank Regiment two years ago. And Whittaker, the driver aboard One-Two, was the youngest associate professor of mathematics at Trinity College, Dublin. He's a bona fide genius. He could be in a quiet comfortable classroom teaching right now instead of being here amongst the mud and the blood," Barnsley shrugged his shoulders. "God knows, none of my men are saints, but they're bound by the notion of duty and honor. They believe they are fighting on the side of right against an evil empire; it's the glue that binds them together."

McLane grunted. Barnsley saw a dark shadow move behind the American officer's eyes. "I imagine, in their own way, your men are fighting this war for the same reasons, right?" the British tankie prompted.

McLane shook his head – not in denial but in despondency, and it was a long while before he finally spoke. His voice was pitched low, and his tone introspective, as if the words were coming from the far end of a long dark passage.

"I don't know why my troops joined the Army," he admitted. "Hell, I can barely remember what motivated me to enlist. We're infantry, Lieutenant. We see the horror of war close up at ground level day in and day out. After a while you become numb, y'know? The blood and the guts and the nightmarish horror of it takes its toll on a man. We're knee deep in that shit every minute of every hour. Eventually a man starts to shut down; starts to shut it out. It's the only way you can keep going. I think each of us enlisted with the same honorable and righteous intentions as your tankers, but this war…" he paused for a moment, searching for the right words but knowing none could ever be adequate. "This war wears you down until all you can think about is surviving one more day… The gruesome horror of close-quarters combat de-humanizes you. Eventually you stop feeling… you stop hoping… at least that's how I've become. An infantryman has to fight every day to survive, but he can't ever survive unaffected…"

They finished drinking in disturbed silence and then stepped somberly back out into the daylight. McLane's face was stony. The crew of Barnsley's tank were packing away the Challenger 2's electric boiling vessel and closing the lid on the brew box that contained extra mugs, spoons, sugar and teabags. The RTR tankies and the Americans stood in small knots, talking in subdued voices.

"We're going to keep pushing north, but we're going across country," Lieutenant Barnsley announced to his tank crews from the doorway of the farm house. "The Russians are overrunning us. We don't know if we still have troops in Elblag, but the odds are against it. That means we're completely cut off from help until we reach Gdansk. Thanks to the cooperation of our American friends," he acknowledged Lieutenant McLane with a gallant bow, "we have a skilled unit of infantry to scout the way ahead. As of right now, they become our eyes and ears."

*

Lieutenant Barnsley spent several minutes shouting across a garbled radio net hissing with static before he threw down his comms set in utter frustration.

"The rest of Cyclops Squadron has been ordered out of Elblag and is retreating on the road to Gdansk with the remains of the Army," the British officer clawed his hands through his hair and sighed as he delivered the bleak news to McLane. "The situation is confused, but there might be Polish recce troops still left in the city – however they won't remain for long."

"What's coming up the highway to our west?"

"Your guess is as good as anybody's," Barnsley said. "There are unconfirmed intelligence reports that enemy T-90s and APCs have been sighted north of a place called Pelplin…"

Neither man knew the town. Barnsley scrambled for the road map and with their heads close together the two officers quickly found the settlement on route E75. McLane made a quick calculation using the width of his thumb as a crude measuring stick. "Less than fifty miles from Gdansk. If they cut across country…"

"Yes," Barnsley winced. If the enemy force on E75 turned east and joined up with the Russians on the road from Paslek, they would be snapped up in the closing jaws. "But right now our first threat are the Russians pressing behind us."

There was not a moment to waste. It could be only a matter of time before the enemy armored column following them found an alternative route across the flooding irrigation channel, or before engineers brought bridging equipment forward.

McLane and his weary Mountaineers struck out from the farm house on foot, trudging across the muddy fields to reconnoiter the crest of a gentle rise that lay three miles north of the farm house. Barnsley threw down the road map and roared at his men to redistribute the remaining ammunition between the three tanks.

Shouts erupted around the farm house and British tankies ran sloshing through the mud, infected with a sudden sense of urgency. McLane could still hear the British Lieutenant barking orders long after they had left the farm house behind.

As the infantrymen patrolled north towards the knoll of high ground, the sun appeared through the blanket of smoke and clouds, bathing the Polish countryside in a soft golden glow. A few miles to their left, sunlight glinted off the surface of the Jezioro Druzno Lake, and a flock of fowl took to sudden flight from out of a clump of long grass in a flurry of beating wings. It was an idyllic scene of tranquil beauty, and for a heartbeat McLane could almost forget about the war and the killing and the chaos. The ground beneath the soldiers' boots was rich farmland heavy with rows of low green flowering plants that stretched all the way to the far crest. He presumed the long ranks of plants they were wading through were crops that would never be harvested. Rifleman Scully, walking close to McLane agreed. "They're potatoes, sir," she offered helpfully. "This part of Poland has good soil, and we're right in the middle of the European growing season."

"You know about farming?"

Scully smiled. "I'm a third generation Idaho farm girl," she said proudly. When she smiled the cuts on her cheek and lip split, trickling fresh blood that she cuffed away with the sleeve of her uniform.

They reached the rise of the knoll at last and cautiously crawled to the crest on their stomachs. McLane pulled the binoculars to his eyes and spent a full minute scanning the terrain ahead.

Before them the ground dipped into a gentle valley, bordered on all sides by rolling tree-covered hills that were hazed grey by smoke and distance. The ground undulated in a number of irregular folds, each small depression studded with trees as though they followed some natural watercourse. Here and there McLane saw wire farm fences, and down in the valley floor, set on a clearing of muddy ground, was another cluster of farm buildings. He saw an abandoned tractor parked in front of a barn and there were deep muddy tire tracks winding their way from the buildings that reached all the way to the far skyline.

McLane swept the binoculars west and then east but saw no movement on the horizon, nothing to cause alarm. He lay unmoving for another twenty seconds with the sun warm on his back before he finally pushed himself upright.

"Move out."

The Mountaineers came to their feet and began the long trudge down the gentle slope. They clambered over a low stone fence and into a meadow of long grass sprinkled with splashes of colorful wildflowers. A grove of low stunted trees grew to the west filled with raucous screeching birds.

McLane's kit thumped and flapped around his waist as he lengthened his stride.

"Does your family still work the potato farm?" he asked Scully offhandedly. In truth he was not listening; instead, he was scanning the far ridge. The distant hills were woven with dense patches of forest and sprinkled with more isolated buildings.

"My grandfather is eighty-three now, but he did –"

What Scully's octogenarian grandfather did remained a mystery, because quite suddenly all of McLane's focus was on the distance. He stopped and stood utterly still.

"Lieutenant!" Sergeant Block looked sideways.

"I see them." For another heartbeat McLane stood frozen to the spot. Then he reeled around his mind a stunned blur, for on the northern skyline, dashing down the slope of the far hill on a trail of rising dust, were armored personnel carriers.

The Russians had cut them off from Elblag.

*

McLane and Sergeant Block exchanged glances. The look in the veteran Sergeant's eyes was the closest to fear McLane had ever seen in him. The Lieutenant's face flushed with sudden debilitating panic.

"Lieutenant…"

McLane shook himself and forced his mind to assess the options. The farm where the Challenger 2 tanks waited was more than three miles behind them on the far side of the crest and across cultivated farm fields. The farmstead he could see down on the valley floor was closer – maybe a mile – but to reach the safety of those buildings meant running *towards* the approaching APCs.

Had they been seen, he wondered? Was there still a chance to hide and evade detection until the enemy had cleared the area?

No. The Russian APCs were coming down the far slope at speed and with purpose.

The Americans were caught in grassy fields without obstacles or cover that would restrict the enemy's movement, and there was no place to hide that the Russians couldn't reach…

Still, he hesitated.

"Lieutenant…"

McLane aimed a long burst of automatic fire into the low smoke-filled sky and then pulled the pin on a grenade. He spun on his heel and threw the grenade as far back up the slope as he could. The grenade exploded with a muffled *'crump!'* and an eruption of smoke and flashing flame. He hoped the frantic sounds of echoing gunfire and explosions would carry beyond the crest to alert the British tank crews to their desperate need for assistance.

"Now run!"

The five soldiers broke into a frantic dash, lifting their legs high in the long grass, their arms pumping as they swarmed down the slope of the grassy hill.

"What are we doing, sir?" Sergeant Block, grim-faced, caught up with McLane who was making a bee-line for the cluster of farm buildings in the valley's floor.

"We're making for the farm house," he pointed as he ran, his face wrenched with the effort to drive his legs through the grass.

"What if it's filled with Russians?" Sergeant Block asked with rising alarm.

"It's not."

"How do you know?"

"Because if it was, we'd be dead by now!"

Sergeant Block peered ahead, past the knot of buildings, to the Russian APCs that were dashing down the far slope, drawing quickly closer. There were three mud-spattered BMP-2s in the group, advancing in a column. Each vehicle mounted a 30mm autocannon in its turret and carried a handful of infantry in its elongated steel hull.

"What about the Brits?" Block was breathing hard, the strain etched across his face.

"We would never make it back to the farm before the Russians caught us and cut us down. We'll just have to trust that the tanks will come looking for us."

Sergeant Block leaped a gnarled bush like a steeplechaser and grunted as he landed, not slowing his step. He threw a glance over his shoulder and saw the three infantrymen pounding the ground close behind him. They were ragged with near exhaustion.

McLane's mind was a whirl of calculations and frantic panic as he ran on. The farmstead comprised three buildings arranged in an open rectangle, with the long stone farmstead bracketed at one end by a horse stable and at the other end by two small stone sheds that might have been storage buildings for machinery or produce. The open side of the rectangle was defined by a waist-high stone wall and an open gate. In the courtyard, close to one of the storage buildings, stood an ancient tractor, sagging on tired suspension and caked brown with mud. It was a bad place to defend – especially against a combined attack from armor and infantry. There were too many blind spots, and too much wall space to secure with only a handful of riflemen. Doubts assailed him as he ran on, now too committed to turn back or seek any other alternatives. They must simply reach the main farm building and fight like berserkers because there was nothing else left to do.

"Run!" he turned and bellowed. He was angry with himself; furious that he had been caught in the open, completely vulnerable. As he pounded on towards the farm house he cursed his failure to study the far ridge more carefully before committing his men to the gentle valley, admonishing himself ruthlessly for plunging them all into fresh danger. "Run!"

The infantrymen ran. Driving through the long tufts of straggling grass was like wading out into the surf of a beach. Private Mallinson stumbled, rolled and somehow regained his feet without losing stride, his helmet flopping down over his eyes and his face wrenched in a rictus of effort. Gardiner and Scully ran on legs made of rubber, their jaws hanging slack as they gulped for air under the oppressive weight of their kit and ammunition. Even Sergeant Block had reached the ragged edge, his breath coming in great punching gasps.

Over the pounding sound of his heart slamming inside his chest, McLane heard the snarl of diesel engines and then saw the three Russian armored personnel carriers emerge through a veil of high shrubs. They were off the slope and now and had reached the valley floor, perhaps just a thousand yards from the farm house. McLane imagined the vehicle commanders studying the small knot of Americans from the viewing prisms in their turrets as the drivers accelerated across the flat ground. In the back of each vehicle a squad of Russian infantry would be checking their weapons, tightening body armor and snatching for spare magazines of ammunition. They would be well rested and brimming with confidence.

"Everyone into the main building!" McLane bellowed as the Mountaineers at last reached the open wrought iron gate set into the stone fence and went pounding across the boggy courtyard. Private Gardiner was first to the farm house. He smashed in the front door with the heel of his boot. Sergeant Block dragged rifleman Scully inside and then McLane wrenched Mallinson by the elbow and shoved him through the opening. The Lieutenant turned on the threshold to cover his men and saw the closest Russian BMP coming on fast.

McLane stepped backwards over the doorsill. "Close it!"

Sergeant Block slammed the door shut. It was flimsy and ill fitting. It looked like an old re-purposed barn door. Block put his shoulder to the weather-warped planks and grunted.

McLane found himself in a living area with passageways running left and right. At the end of one passage, he could see a kitchen and at the end of the other were bedrooms, their doors hanging open and discarded bundles of clothes strewn across the floor. The interior of the farm house smelled of stale cooking grease and garlic.

"Sergeant! Take Mallinson and cover those bedrooms and the rear of the building. Scully and Gardiner, on me!"

The farm house had long been abandoned and most of the furniture removed by the fleeing owners. What remained was little more than a gloomy shell. The windows were small and the ceiling low. McLane posted Scully in front of a window on one side of the doorway and Gardiner at a window on the other side. He ducked down behind a section of wall and peered out into the courtyard.

The Russian BMP-2s came charging across the valley floor. McLane saw great flurries of mud and clods of grass thrown up by the churning tracks. The APCs were slewing sideways in the soft boggy ground as they raced towards the farm house, heedless of any danger. They slammed to a halt two hundred yards short of the main building, on the far side of the low stone fence.

The BMP-2s were menacing armored beasts, their angular front hull like an avalanche of steel, their low-profile turrets turning towards the wall of the farm house. They were painted in a woodland camouflage of olive green and brown. Their steel tracks were caked with mud and grass, their hulls streaked with the dirt and grime accumulated from endless days of hard combat.

McLane felt a frisson of fear turn the sweat on his back cold as ice.

For what we are about to receive...

The hatch-like rear doors on the three vehicles swung open and Russian infantry spilled out, marshaling in the lee of the steel troop carriers to protect themselves from American fire. There was a pause of almost sixty seconds as officers arranged the troops while in the gloom of the farm house the American riflemen fretted anxiously. They were trapped like rats without any chance of escape, and they were outnumbered and overwhelmed by superior firepower.

"Get behind something solid and stay there!" McLane's voice of warning carried down the passageway.

May the Lord make us truly thankful...

The 30mm Shipunov 2A42 autocannons mounted atop the turrets of each Russian armored personnel carrier opened fire on the farm house with an earth-shattering roar, and a seething frenzy of dust and debris and destruction. The savage flail of heavy cannon fire tore the old farm house's walls to pieces, crumbling stonework and tearing huge chunks from the rustic masonry. Windows imploded, showering the interior with shattered glass. The front door splintered and then broke into a thousand pieces. Bullets stitched the interior walls and blasted through bedding and kitchen benches. McLane tucked himself into a tight ball on the floor and covered his head with his hands as the entire building shook and trembled. The air became choking with dust and still the Russian autocannons continued firing until McLane's ears were ringing and the whole building seemed on the brink of demolition.

When the turret-mounted guns at last stopped firing, the dreadful aftermath of the maelstrom was eerie and ominous. Dust swirled in drifts and McLane could smell smoke. The interior of the farm house had been chewed to tattered pieces. Part of the building's rear wall caved in, leaving a gap near the roof through which watery sunlight filtered through. The floor around him was strewn with broken glass and crumbled masonry chunks, some the size of his fist.

"Anybody hit?" he shouted the question.

"We're good!" Sergeant Block's voice carried down the passage, between coughing gasps of breath.

McLane looked left and right. Scully lay curled up on the floor, her head and shoulders powdered white by masonry dust and fallen debris. A jagged slab of ceiling plaster the size of a tabletop had collapsed on her. Private Gardiner lay with his face pressed to the wall, and his M4 in his trembling hand. He shook and gasped for breath like a man on the verge of a panic attack. McLane's voice cut across the fraught silence. "Gardiner! Gardiner!" he had to call twice to get the young rifleman's attention. Gardiner's eyes had a wild, panicked cast. "Calm the fuck down!"

The rifleman took a couple of deep gulps of dust-thick air, and the hysteria in his expression began to fade. He spat out a mouthful of grit and nodded, chastened and embarrassed.

McLane poked his head cautiously above the window sill and heard the voices of Russian officers bellowing at their men. The troops were still sheltered behind the steel bulk of the APCs. McLane couldn't understand the language, but he recognized the tone and what it was building up to.

"They're gearing up for an attack," he called down the passageway.

"Balls to the wall, riflemen!" Sergeant Block shouted from the far bedroom, hyping up the troops. The Mountaineers scrambled to the windows and took up firing positions. The Russian BMP-2s were two hundred yards back from the farm house wall. They opened fire again just as the infantry hiding behind them burst from cover, fanning out and charging towards the stone building in a ragged wave. The charge was not pressed home with any determination. The Russian infantry seemed intent on covering just the ground between their armored vehicles and the shelter of the low stone wall. They ran doubled over, their heavy boots sloshing and splashing through the track-churned grass. Some of the men were shouting as they charged, their teeth bared and their faces pale white with fear. Behind them, their officers drove the infantry forward, gesturing frantically for them to clamber over the wall and surge through the gate, then push on to the front door of the building.

The APCs fired at the farm house, stitching the ravaged walls with a fury of autocannon rounds until their infantry spread out in front of them and the guns were forced to fall silent.

"Fire!" McLane roared.

He took aim on an enemy soldier amidst the press of surging bodies and felt the M4 kick against his shoulder. The Russian took two rounds full in the face. His head snapped back, turned to gruesome bloody mush in an instant. He fell on his back in the mud. The soldier running beside the dead man stopped, looked down at his slaughtered comrade and vomited over his boots. McLane shot him in the side of the head.

"Fire!"

Rifleman Scully picked out an enemy soldier running under the burden of a heavy machine gun. He was a huge bear of a man with bulging biceps and a bull neck. She trapped him in her sights and fired three times, striking the man twice. The first bullet seemed to be deflected by the body armor the Russian wore strapped across his chest. The second round struck him under the heavy bone of his jaw. A bright gushing fountain of blood spurted into the bullet-torn air. The Russian staggered and then sagged forward into the mud, the machine gun still cradled in his arms. The lower section of his face had been shot away. He made a strangled incoherent sound of pain and died choking on his own blood.

"Fire!"

Four more Russians went down to well-aimed shots before the enemy soldiers reached the sanctuary of the stone wall and began to fire back. Over the ragged sounds of gunfire McLane could still hear a Russian officer cajoling his men and berating them for their cowardice. He sought out the source of the strident voice and spotted a Russian soldier wearing officer's epaulets. He had crouched behind the wall, close to the open gate. McLane took careful aim and waited for the Russian to raise his head. He fired, but missed.

The Russian scrambled back behind the stone wall and his baying shouts reached an indignant feverish pitch.

McLane switched aim to another Russian who was kneeling behind the wall, hastily unfolding the bipod legs of a machine gun. The man's head bobbed up from behind cover and McLane snapped off a reflexive shot. The bullet whined off the stone fence an inch from the Russian's left ear. "Bastard!" he cursed another precious bullet wasted.

Sergeant Block came swarming down the passageway from the front bedroom, bent double to keep from revealing himself as he passed each window, his M4 in his hand and a look of deep concern on his craggy face. He crouched low next to McLane.

"Lieutenant, we gotta get out of here. Any minute now those fuckers are going to realize we ain't got shit to fight them with and they're going to bulldoze down these walls with their fuckin' troop carriers and run right over us."

McLane grunted, but before he could reply there was a sudden panicked shout from Private Mallinson in the far bedroom, then a furious fusillade of enemy gunfire that sawed and crashed against the rear wall of the farm house. McLane and Block charged along the passage and into a madness of shouting and snarling automatic gunfire. Private Mallinson sat slumped against the far bedroom wall, firing his M4 one handed with the stock of the weapon braced under his armpit, his left arm awash with blood and dangling useless by his side. There was more blood splashed over the bedroom walls and along the window sill where three Russian soldiers were trying to clamber in through the shattered glass.

McLane and Block opened fire from the bedroom doorway, shooting from the hip and spraying the window with a hail of spitting lead. The room filled with smoke and swirling debris. The two Russians jammed in the window were thrown backwards by the fusillade, but in the background, McLane saw more Russians were on the move. Block went to the window and fired into the mass of bodies. On the ground outside the window the two wounded Russians were writhing in pain and bleeding from multiple wounds. One of them reached a trembling, bloody hand for his weapon. The American Sergeant did not hesitate; he shot both enemy soldiers dead.

Mallinson had been hit in the arm. McLane hastily dressed the wound and between them Block and the Lieutenant dragged the bleeding rifleman down the passageway.

"We're pulling out," McLane declared. Behind the shelter of the stone fence, he spotted another group of Russian soldiers skirting sideways. They were firing wildly as they ran, moving towards the stables building. "We'll take our chances in the fields."

One of the BMP-2s autocannons resumed firing and a hail of empty shell casings spewed onto the ground. The bullets sawed across the front wall of the farm house, peppering the smashed front doorway. McLane cringed and ducked his head low on his shoulders. "On me, okay? On me! Everyone goes out through the bedroom window but Scully," he stared at the smoke-stained and bloody faces pressed close to his. "Scully, you stay. You're the last man, understand?"

"I'm last man," Scully repeated. "I'm last man."

Sergeant Block set himself to be first out through the shattered window. Mallinson was pale-faced and looked like he was going into shock. He was on his feet but swaying like a drunk. Gardiner pushed him back towards the bedroom. "I'm shot! I'm shot!" Mallinson shouted, his shrieking voice adding to the chaos and confusion. Sergeant Block snarled at the rifleman to shut the fuck up and then prepared himself to burst from the building on what he knew would be a suicidal escape attempt.

"Wait!" It was Lieutenant McLane, his voice urgent and so loud it seemed to freeze time for an instant.

Because a new sound had suddenly joined the clamor of battle.

From his tank's position hull down behind the crest of the ridge in the middle of the potato field, Lieutenant Barnsley used his thumb controller to lay his CPS aiming mark on the closest Russian BMP-2 and barked the order his crew had been anticipating.

"Fin, APC!" he called. He stabbed the 'Align' switch on his commander's control handle with his finger and the Challenger 2's turret moved a fraction of an inch, aligning with the CPS aiming mark. The tank's loader thrust a HESH round into the open breech.

"Loaded!"

The tank's gunner checked his GPS and called out, "On!" to confirm the target.

The range was just over a thousand yards. The gunner waited a split-second for the tank's fire control system to make its calculations and then shouted, "Firing!" The huge main gun roared and for a second the tank disappeared behind the fireball of its muzzle flash.

Inside the Challenger's vast steel turret, the British Lieutenant tracked the low-velocity HESH shot through his viewing prisms. Down on the valley floor one of the Russian armored personnel carriers suddenly erupted in a spectacular explosion of flames and smoke and twisted metal fragments.

The explosion that destroyed the APC was shockingly massive. Heat and roiling flames washed over the battlefield, slamming Russian soldiers off their feet and engulfing the entire farm complex in a vast black column of smoke.

"Finish the bastards off!" Barnsley spoke across the Troop net. The other two Challenger tanks fired a few seconds later, one after the other. In a matter of moments all three of the enemy BMP-2s were flaming ruins. More than half the Russian infantry were killed or severely injured in the three massive explosions. They writhed in the mud screaming from gruesome wounds. One soldier lay in the long grass, his knees drawn up, trying to push his entrails back inside his stomach with blood-slippery hands. He was sobbing with the effort, making small whimpering noises of excruciating pain as the flies feasted greedily on the gore. Beside him a man had been decapitated by a chunk of white-hot shrapnel. Others were bleeding from fatal wounds or had been cruelly burned in the savage tempest.

The Mountaineers came from within the ruined farm house with the wonder of relief etched on their haggard faces. McLane walked amidst the carnage grim-faced, his features frozen into a rictus-like grimace as he inspected the enemy dead. A few of the surviving Russians had fled to the north on foot, but most were here, dead or dying in the mud. One man had both his legs blown off below the knees, the tattered flesh protruding shards of white broken bone as the soldier tried vainly to staunch the bleeding. He looked up into McLane's face, a silent plea for mercy in his eyes. McLane walked on. He found the Russian officer he had fired at near the stone wall. The man's body had been slashed by at least a dozen steel shrapnel fragments. There was spattered blood dashed against the wall and thick on the ground around the officer's mangled corpse. McLane nudged the prone body with the toe of his boot just to be certain he was dead.

A shot rang out and McLane looked up to see Sergeant Block standing over a Russian body with the muzzle of his M4 pressed to the corpse's head. McLane said nothing. He felt numbed and dazed, his senses oversaturated with the gore and the gruesome images of war. He turned to the south and watched the three Challenger 2s approach. They came on cautiously as they traversed the uneven ground, and then braked to a halt on the mud trail left by the BMP-2s. The turret hatch on Barnsley's tank swung open and the

Lieutenant emerged, red splotches of color on his pale cheeks and a frown on his brow.

"You seem to have a knack of finding trouble, Lieutenant McLane," the Englishman understated dryly. "Even a simple recce mission ends in bloodshed."

"I'm just the right guy whose always in the wrong place," McLane said, and then took another slow look around the carnage that surrounded him. The mud on his boots was stained with Russian blood and in the background he could still hear the feeble dying groans of enemy soldiers who were gasping their last breaths. He shut out the horror and cleared his mind. "I think we need another plan. Softly, softly, catchee monkey ain't gonna work. If the Russians didn't know we were running loose beforehand, they certainly will now. Those BMP-2s must have a command element somewhere nearby. There's probably already a dozen more APCs on their way to intercept us."

Chapter 7:

The wound to Mallinson's arm proved superficial. One of the British tankies patched the rifleman up and when he winced with the pain of it, Scully and Gardiner scornfully jeered him.

"Will you be alright to fight?" McLane stood over the injured Mallinson while his arm was being bandaged.

"It's just a bloody scratch," the British tankie gave the American Lieutenant a cheeky grin and answered in place of Mallinson. "I've hurt myself worse with a razor blade." He gave the rifleman's arm a short jab that made Mallinson grimace in fresh agony and then packed away the tank's first aid kit. "I'll send you the bill."

The Mountaineers clambered wearily onto the tanks. McLane and Barnsley met beside the splintered farm house's front door. Barnsley had the road map in his hands.

McLane glanced sideways at the British tank commander whose pale unshaven face looked strained. "Are we going to make a run for it?"

"It's the only option we have left," Barnsley spread the map out and gnawed thoughtfully on his bottom lip. "Something tells me we've used up all our luck."

McLane grunted. "How far is it to Elblag?"

"Ten kilometers by road… but those roads will be choked with abandoned vehicles, bodies and maybe Russians by now."

McLane felt unaccountably exhausted, his nerves stretched out on the rack of unrelenting danger. With a tremendous effort of resolve, he forced his fatigued mind to think. "So we keep heading north cross country?"

"It will probably be faster," Lieutenant Barnsley opined. He offered the creased and stained map to McLane and traced a line with his finger. "If we follow the eastern bank of this lake far enough north, it will eventually open into the Elblag River. Once we meet the river, we can follow it all the way to this bridge on the south western outskirts of the city. It's the main route to Gdansk. If there are Allied troops still anywhere near Elblag, they'll be at that bridge crossing."

"What if the bridge has already been destroyed?"

Barnsley looked pained. He made a troubled face. "There are a couple of other minor bridges in the center of the city…" he muttered vaguely.

There was nothing more to say. The two men looked at each other, both aware that their situation grew more hopeless and more desperate by the minute. "Okay," McLane nodded and clenched his jaw. "Then let's rock 'n' roll."

It was afternoon now and the cloud cover and thick blanket of smoke made the world a cold, gloomy place. A cruel, chill wind came hunting from the southeast so the weary soldiers slumped on the back of the tanks shivered in misery. Overhead, and obscured from view by the cloud cover, jet fighters streaked across the sky, the whine of their roaring engines a constant remined of how close danger loomed.

McLane and Sergeant Block sat close together on the Challenger 2s rear deck plate, neither man attempting to speak above the snarl of the huge powerpack. Their heads rocked on their shoulders as the tanks jounced and slewed for traction in the mud. McLane felt his eyes growing heavy and had to fight to remain awake. To distract himself, he peered past the tank's turret.

In the distance and smudged by smoke, he saw the dull grey silhouette of city buildings, their outline ragged against the low sullen sky. He turned and looked east and after a long moment he thought he detected the straight line of the highway, drawn like a thin black scar across the skyline. He narrowed his eyes and watched the highway for movement as the tanks drew inexorably closer, but saw nothing.

Sergeant Block grabbed at his shoulder to get his attention and pointed wordlessly to a grove of trees the tanks were passing.

In the midst of the woods was the burned-out carcass of a downed American F-15 Eagle fighter. McLane could see the aircraft's Base Code and the three digit serial number on the remains of the jet's twin tailfins. The plane had ploughed into the stand of trees and disintegrated on impact. Part of the airframe was blackened by fire, and several of the surrounding trees had been flattened by the thundering impact. Twisted chunks of wreckage were strewn across the muddy ground for hundreds of yards in every direction, and in the top of a tree McLane saw part of a wing hanging in the branches. The wreckage appeared several days old.

McLane continued to peer at the downed fighter jet until the three Challengers suddenly began to trundle up a gradual incline.

They had reached the highway that bypassed Elblag.

The Challengers mounted the causeway and pulled onto the highway, facing north. A mile ahead they could see the bridge over the Elblag River and to their right, behind a low fringe of riverbank trees, stood the silhouetted skyline of the city, smoldering smoke. The skyline was dominated by a tall tower and spire that McLane guessed was some kind of historic church. Somehow the building had defied the Russian bombers while the city around it had been pulverized to grey rubble. The river that wound beneath the bridge and then through the city was grey with dust and lumpen with floating debris.

The highway ran two lanes wide in both directions – but all four lanes were littered with the ruins of an Army in retreat. Barnsley's Challenger nudged aside the mangled ruins of a burned-out British Army truck and nosed cautiously forward. There were dead bodies on the side of the road and dead livestock, their bloated corpses overblown with flies and oozing maggots. The stench of corruption caught putrid and oily in the back of McLane's throat. An overturned cart of rotting vegetables had spilled ruined food across the blacktop and there were hundreds of crows on the steel guiderails, screeching protest at the tank's interruption. A car by the side of the road was riddled with bullet holes, its windows smashed.

Lieutenant Barnsley thrust his head out through the open commander's hatch of his Challenger's turret and peered north with binoculars pressed to his eyes. The bridge crossing appeared to be barricaded by a jumble of waist-high concrete jersey barriers.

The British tank commander motioned to McLane who leaned his head forward so he could hear the message above the deafening whine of the tank's powerpack. Barnsley was smiling his disbelieving relief, his voice full of self-congratulations. "We made it, and the bridge is intact. Now I just need you and your men to scout forward to check for IEDs and ambushes. Once we get the all clear we'll transit the crossing, then find a place from where we can destroy the bridge. After we've done that, there will be diddly-squat the Russians at our rear can do to catch us."

Destroying the bridge wouldn't eliminate the danger that the Russian column advancing to the west might cut across northern Poland and intercept their route to Gdansk, but it would put paid to any further pursuit from those enemy troops swarming towards them from the south. McLane nodded and felt himself smiling. The ordeal was almost over…

The Mountaineers scrambled off the tanks and went forward quickly. Lieutenant Barnsley turned in his hatch and peered south, searching the distance for the telltale signs of approaching Russian troops. The sky was so dark with black smoke that the world had been plunged into an eerie unnatural twilight.

The Mountaineers fanned out across the two northbound lanes of the highway and went forward cautiously. The air was thick with swarming flies and the stench of corruption was so nauseatingly foul that it was hard to draw breath. The litter-strewn blacktop had been spattered with dry blood, dead bodies and abandoned cars. McLane saw a small baby-sized shape lying face down in the gutter. He peered at it for several seconds before he realized, with relief, that it was an abandoned child's doll.

A sudden shout from the far side of a concrete barrier brought his head snapping up and his soldiers on instant alert.

"Put your hands up, Russian bastards!" The voice was heavily accented. The speaker sounded young and nervous.

"We're not Russians. We're Americans."

There was a moment of confused suspicious silence from the far side of the barricade before the voice called out again.

"I don't believe you."

"I don't give a shit," McLane's temper flared irritably. "I'm speaking fuckin' American, god-damn it. Now put your gun down and quit jerkin' me around."

He strode boldly towards the road-block. Behind the concrete barricade he saw three fresh-faced soldiers in what appeared to be standard Polish Army uniforms. They were pointing FB Beryl assault rifles at his chest. "I'm Lieutenant Simon McLane, 1st Platoon, Charlie Company, 2nd Battalion of the 10th Mountain Division. Who are you?"

The three young Polish soldiers lowered their weapons. One of them spoke up. He looked to McLane like he was still too young to shave. He had dark nervous eyes and ginger hair sprouting from beneath the rim of his helmet.

"We're Polish Engineer Corps," the young sapper's English was so heavily accented that McLane had trouble understanding. He seemed uncertain if he should salute the American officer. "We retreated north with the rest of the Army from our base in Kazun Nowy, northwest of Warsaw. We have orders to blow the bridge."

"When?"

"At sunset."

"You haven't got that long. The Russians are right behind us," McLane told the Polish sapper.

The young man gaped in shock and panic. "For certain?"

"Yes! For fuckin' certain!" Exhaustion made McLane indignant. "There's at least a Company of BMP-2s close behind us and probably a couple of hundred T-90 MBTs heading your way." As if to verify his claims, the far-off rumble of Russian artillery sounded on the soft fluttering breeze. It was a noise like rolling thunder underlaid by a tenuous smaller sound that might have been diesel engines. "Where is your Sergeant?"

"He's in the city, supervising the demolition of some smaller bridges across the river," the young Polish soldier's cheeks began to flush red as he suddenly realized the peril of his position. His gaze flicked nervously past McLane's shoulder as though he might at any moment see the entire Russian Army appear on the southern skyline.

"And your Captain?"

"He is to the north," the sapper turned and pointed into the far distance. "He's at the Nogat."

"The Nogat?"

"The Nogat River," the young Polish sapper explained. "He is supervising the demolition of the bridge there."

"There's *another* bridge?"

"Of course," the sapper said. "It's the critical bridge between here and the Vistula River."

"I thought *this* was the critical bridge," McLane's temper, already on a short fuse, sparked with bitter frustration.

"No," the sapper shook his head. "There are too many nearby routes the Russians can take across the Elblag. We can't possibly destroy them all. But the bridge over the Nogat is the only crossing for miles in any direction of the main road."

"How far away is this bridge across the Nogat?"

"About ten kilometers further north."

"And when is it scheduled for demolition?"

"Sunset," the sapper said.

McLane stared. For a few seconds he was too shocked to speak, but then he exploded in exasperation. "Christ!"

He wheeled around and stared up at the brooding sky. It seemed to him that darkness was just minutes away. He turned on his heel and started sprinting back towards the waiting Challengers, his men running alongside him. He shouted towards Lieutenant Barnsley as he ran. "We're still not safe. There's another fuckin' bridge we have to cross!"

*

The British tanks needed fuel. "There is a depot on the eastern outskirts of Elblag," the young Polish sapper offered helpfully. "It belonged to a French unit that garrisoned the city before the retreat from Warsaw."

"Where are the French?"

"They're all to the north. They fled with the defeated armies."

The streets of Elblag were a deserted ruin of rubble and fire-charred remains. Most of the local inhabitants had evacuated their homes when news first reached them that Warsaw had fallen to the Russians, and the Allied armies were retreating towards Gdansk. Now there was just a few barking, starving dogs in the streets as the three Challenger 2 tanks trundled through the maze of alleyways in search of the French supply depot.

The buildings the French Army had occupied had been looted, but a CaRaPACE armored fuel tanker truck and three Renault Kerax heavy duty transport trucks were still parked in the motor pool. McLane and his men left the refueling task to the British tankies and instead scouted the ruins along the city's riverbank.

There was an eerie oppressive stillness to the city that McLane found unsettling. There were looted and naked bodies strewn along the watercourse. The dead lay scattered in tortured poses, their flesh picked to the bone by the carrion birds and their corpses swollen and turning purple. There were more dead in the shadow-struck alleys; several had been killed by the Russian bombing raids, others had been crushed in the ruined buildings when they had collapsed. Dogs had gnawed and mauled some of the bodies.

McLane walked to the end of a narrow lane and peered south. He had a view to the outskirts of the city. The air was still, the sky overhead made brooding and sullen by the onset of dusk. The world crushed under an oppressive silence as though cringing from imminent carnage and chaos.

He scratched at the unshaven stubble across his jaw and then blinked in sudden shock and gut-sick dread. On the skyline the imminent carnage and chaos the world had been cowering from suddenly appeared on the distant skyline in the form of a column of Russian tanks.

"Christ!" Then McLane was turning and shouting, his voice urgent as he broke into a desperate run. "Get back to the Challengers on the double. Move it Mountaineers!"

*

The Russians converged on Elblag from the south and the east. In the vanguard were units of BMP-2 armored personnel carriers, scouting ahead of the main armored column. Like the whiskers of a cat, they roamed across the farmlands to the east of the city 'feeling' for signs of enemy resistance. Behind them, and formed up in two columns across the highway, followed a Battalion of T-90 main battle tanks, and behind them were lined rank upon rank of BMPs to transport the motor rifle Companies.

In the sky forward of the battle force maneuvered three long-range unmanned aerial vehicles. The Orlan-10 reconnaissance drones dropped out of cloud cover and came arrowing across the city's outskirts then turned west towards the bridge.

It took ninety seconds for McLane and the small band of infantrymen to return to the French military depot. The British crewmen were hastily finishing off the refueling process, their eyes anxiously on the sky as they topped off the thirsty fuel tanks. The Challenger 2s powerpacks roared to life and the soldiers scrambled aboard.

"We have to get to the bridge before the Russians arrive!"

The Challengers re-traced their route back through the city streets. Through the bomb-damaged ruins, McLane kept his eyes on the sky to the south. A Russian drone was circling high overhead, fading in and out of view behind drifting smoke skeins. When the Challengers burst into the clear and the landscape around them flattened, McLane stared south anxiously and saw the nearest BMPs were less than two thousand yards away. They were still screening the advance of the T-90s but as he watched the Russian APCs suddenly changed course and jounced off the road, making for the eastern outskirts of the city. The maneuver was performed with the drama of a theater curtain being drawn aside, revealing the phalanx of Russian MBTs drawn across the highway and surging towards them.

The Challengers reached the highway entry-ramp and rejoined the main road north on the far side of the bridge. The three young Polish sappers were fleeing towards a Polish Army Skorpion four-wheel drive.

"Why aren't you blowing up the bridge?" McLane jumped down from the back of Lieutenant Barnsley's Challenger and seized one of the sappers by the front of his tunic. The young man was wild-eyed and trembling. McLane cuffed the soldier hard behind the ear and his head shook on his shoulders. "Why aren't you destroying the fucking bridge?" he shouted in the sapper's face.

"Our Sergeant," the Polish Private made a helpless gesture and stammered out a response. "He has not returned. We have no orders…"

"I'm giving you the fucking orders!" McLane roared. "Blow the god-damned thing up!"

"We can't!" the sapper struggled to wrench himself free of McLane's grip. On the far side of the road his two companions were tumbling inside the Skorpion. The engine roared. The sapper broke McLane's grip and went scampering across the blacktop. McLane thought about shooting the bastard but decided he would soon need every bullet.

He swore bitterly after the sapper and then a new sound on the air seized his attention. He turned and lifted his eyes skyward, filled with ominous foreboding.

Far behind the advancing column of enemy armor, six dark dots suddenly appeared from over the horizon. They hung in the sky, low above the landscape, their silhouettes smudged by smoke and a background of tree clutter. McLane watched the specks gradually grow larger and take on menacing shape as the sound of their approach became a clattering thunder that beat against the cloud-filled sky. The six M1-8TV (Hip-E) assault helicopters were flying directly for the bridge, their cargo bays crammed with two dozen elite Russian paratroopers and their external hard points bristling S-5 rockets. The bellies of the helicopters scraped the treetops as they swooped towards the Elblag River. McLane knew with absolute certainty what the menacing thunder in the air presaged; the Russians were launching an assault to seize the bridge before it could be destroyed.

He ran back to the Challenger, climbed aboard the stern deck and hammered the butt of his M4 against the commander's turret hatch. It swung open and Lieutenant Bradley's harried face emerged from the gloomy interior.

"Can you destroy the bridge with a HESH round?"

"It's a flat stretch of highway," the tank commander protested. "We'd have to find a firing location from inside the city and hit it broadside."

"There isn't time!"

"Then it isn't possible."

"Fuck!" McLane tried to guess how long before the Russian helicopters reached their position. He figured they had less than two minutes before the entire bridge would be swarming with paratroopers, T-90s and certain death. A sudden sound like a crack of thunder slammed against the sky and a split-second later a round from one of the advancing T-90 tanks landed two hundred yards west of the bridge. The explosion tore a great crater of earth out of the riverbank.

"Fuck!" the American Lieutenant swore again. The three Challengers were scattered across the blacktop, their turrets turned to face the approaching Russian T-90s. The tanks were reversing away from the bridge slowly. Lieutenant Barnsley was acutely aware how exposed his position was. They were on open ground with little cover. He made the decision. "We're pulling out!" he said. "We can't fight the entire bloody

Russian Army, and we can't do a damned thing to destroy the bridge."

McLane slammed his fist against the steel turret in frustration and smeared skin from his knuckles. He could already hear the enemy's BMPs in the city streets, their autocannons blazing away at the empty bomb-ravaged buildings. Any moment they would appear at the on-ramp with a screen of enemy infantry around them and the British tanks would be surrounded.

He nodded his head, galled at how swiftly the prospect of respite had soured into a fresh disaster. The tank's hatches slammed shut and a moment later all three Challenger 2s turned and raced north at high speed like the hounds of Hell were at their heels.

*

It was another twenty grueling minutes on the road north of Elblag before the bridge over the Nogat River loomed on the horizon. The tanks were heading due west towards the sinking sun and the view as the river finally appeared proved unremarkable. All McLane could see from the back deck of the Challenger 2 was a fringe of green trees that stretched across the skyline surrounded by more ploughed farm fields.

The three tanks slowed and McLane stole an anxious glance back along the highway, expecting Russian T-90s to appear at any moment. The route behind them was empty, but the sounds of distant helicopters still beat against the air, coming and then fading on the fluky wind.

The road ahead kinked left, narrowing to two lanes as it reached an area of dense woodlands, then kinked right again on its approach to the bridge. As the tanks rounded the final sweeping bend, they ran headlong into a Polish Army road-block. There were three KTO Rosomak Wolverine armored personnel carriers parked broadside across the blacktop, their turrets turned to face the approach and a soldier in each vehicle manning the Bushmaster II 30mm cannon.

On the shoulder of the highway, and set back inside the tree line that fringed the approach to the bridge, Polish infantry armed with Javelin anti-tank weapons were concealed in deep foxholes supported by a Platoon of armed light infantry.

Lieutenant Barnsley halted his Challenger in the middle of the highway two hundred yards short of the road-block and climbed down from his turret. Together he and McLane strode forward.

A hundred yards beyond the Polish APCs the bridge itself was swarming with bustling engineers and littered with a collection of trucks and military four-wheel drives, parked haphazardly across the bridge's span. McLane and Barnsley stopped short of the Wolverines and a Polish officer appeared from the shadow of the trees to intercept them. The young man's face was tense, creased with anxious worry. He had the appearance of a harassed administrator, more comfortable behind a desk than a gun.

"Are you in charge here?" Lieutenant Barnsley made a gesture that embraced the entire scene of frantic activity.

The Polish officer was a Lieutenant. His English was fractured and thickly accented. "Captain Augustyniak from the Corps of Polish Engineers commands. I am Lieutenant Lewandowski."

"Can you tell us why your APCs are blocking the highway, Lieutenant?" Barnsley kept his voice civil although he was acutely aware there was not a second to waste with politics or pleasantries. At any moment the Russian armored column could appear on the road behind them and launch an attack. "We are British tanks and American infantry. We've been fighting a rearguard action against the Russians for the past two days around the town of Paslek. We need to get across the bridge and rejoin our armies at Gdansk."

"No cross bridge," the Polish junior officer said sharply and shook his head. "It is still being mined with demolition charges."

"You mean it's not rigged to blow yet?" McLane's face turned aghast with horror. "The entire fucking Russian Army is right up our ass, buddy. In ten minutes from now this place is going to be crawling with enemy tanks and paratroopers. If that bridge isn't destroyed before they get here, we're all fucked."

The Polish Lieutenant flinched in the face of McLane's expletive-loaded tirade. He glanced over his shoulder, evidently found who he was searching for, then drew himself stiffly to attention. "I will get Captain. He will explain."

For three interminable minutes McLane and Barnsley stood waiting impatiently until the Polish Lieutenant returned with a large-framed Captain in camouflage fatigues. The senior Polish officer wore a thick black moustache in the style of Saddam Hussein and a beret draped low over his right eye at a rakish angle. He came striding forward with a confident, arrogant swagger.

"Piss off with your tanks," the Polish Captain scowled. His English was stilted. He waved his arm as if to shoo away the three seventy-ton main battle tanks.

McLane blinked. He and Lieutenant Barnsley exchanged bewildered glances. McLane's first instinct was to leap on the bastard's chest and tear his throat out – but the British officer spoke up first, choosing diplomacy and reason.

"Captain, we need to cross this bridge, and the bridge needs to be destroyed the moment we reach the far side. The Russian Army is advancing along this road and will be within sight of your position in a matter of minutes."

For a moment longer the Polish Engineers officer's face maintained its arrogant bumptious pout – and then the confident façade crumbled and his expression tuned to one of rising alarm.

"But the Russians cannot come yet. The bridge... the charges..." He turned and roared at the sappers bustling about the cargo trucks in a tirade of staccato Polish. Men were climbing into the bridge's steel girders with C4 explosives trailing lengths of det cord while others hung from the guard rails and men with jackhammers drilled holes in the blacktop for cratering charges. There were more sappers beneath the bridge's span, setting charges around the concrete footers that braced the structure from below. "We are not ready to destroy the bridge."

"Oh, my God," Barnsley groaned wanly.

It was a complete shambles.

McLane and Barnsley exchanged mortified glances. "This is a world class clusterfuck," McLane vented his smoldering frustration. "If the Russians are allowed to seize this bridge intact then the remnants of the Allied Armies still straggling towards Gdansk will be vulnerable. By the time the survivors reach the coast there won't be an army left for NATO to fight with. They'll be slaughtered to a man."

Lieutenant Barnsley trapped his bottom lip between his teeth, spun on his heel and started back at the three remaining tanks of his Troop. Then he lifted his eyes to the smoke-stained sky like he was offering some silent prayer to the gods of war. When he turned back again his features were set, his mind resolved.

"How much time do you need before the bridge is ready for demolition?" he asked the Polish Captain of Engineers.

"Another hour," Captain Augustyniak said. "We will be ready at sunset. Not before."

"An hour," Barnsley repeated. His voice had taken on the tone of a condemned man. "Very well. My tanks will do our best to hold up the enemy and buy you the time you need." Without another word the British Lieutenant marched back down the highway towards the three waiting Challengers. McLane paused at the road-block long enough to press his face close to the Polish Engineer.

"Do you have flares?" McLane snarled the question at the Polish Captain.

"Flares?" the Engineer seemed perplexed. "Yes."

"The moment the bridge is ready to be destroyed, fire a green flare so we know to fall back to safety. Got it?"

The Engineers Officer nodded his head.

McLane started back towards the tanks and his waiting troops. He took ten strides down the center of the highway, then stopped suddenly and turned on his heel. He came back to where the Polish Captain stood and lowered his voice to a hoarse whisper, his temper seething.

"That bridge better be ready to blow in sixty minutes," he snarled, the menace in his voice unmistakable. "Because if it's not, you won't have to worry about being shot by the Russians. I'll fucking kill you myself."

*

"You don't need to be a part of this fight," Lieutenant Barnsley drew McLane to one side of the highway, out of earshot of the waiting tank crews and infantrymen. "You and your unit have done more than your duty demanded. You should get across that bridge and keep marching. Gdansk is fifty kilometers straight ahead."

"We're not going anywhere," McLane said. "It's too goddamned far to walk, and I kind of enjoy riding on the back of a Challenger."

"You have a responsibility to your men to get them to safety…"

"I have a greater responsibility to the rest of the Army that will be slaughtered if we don't hold this bridge."

Barnsley nodded and for a long moment the two men shared a silent look that spoke to the bond of trust they had formed. Sergeant Block appeared behind the British Lieutenant's shoulder.

"Lieutenant McLane? You mind telling me what in the god-damned hell we're doing here, sir?"

"We're making a stand, Sergeant," McLane said grimly.

*

With the decision made the next frantic minutes became a blur of hastily barked orders and furious action. Barnsley ordered his Challengers into the tree line on the edge of the highway to cover the approach to the bridge. Once the tanks were positioned and concealed in deep dappled shadow, the crews dug furiously to reinforce each tank's position with a crude wall of earthworks. McLane sent Scully into the Polish trenches to procure ammunition; the Polish Mod 96 Beryl rifle used the same 5.56mm NATO rounds as the American M4. Scully fell on the hapless Polish infantry platoon like a vulture and returned with her arms full of fresh magazines and her pockets bulging with grenades.

Sergeant Block went deeper into the woods like a bloodhound on the scent, studying the terrain carefully with an experienced soldier's eye. Finally he ordered the Polish infantry to dig a series of new trenches that were positioned to protect the Challengers from an enemy infantry attack through the forest. The Polish Lieutenant sidled up beside McLane and his voice was nervous.

"I… I don't know what to do," the young officer's face was flushed with acute embarrassment.

"There's nothing to do right now except grab a trenching tool and dig," the American explained curtly. He turned and strode to the edge of the highway and peered west, his eyes following the course of the Nogat. The farm fields beside the tree-lined riverbank would make an ideal LZ for Russian helicopters. From those fields, the ground rose in a gentle grassy incline up to the side of the highway. If the Russians were able to get paratroopers on the ground, they could storm the bridge and take the British tank positions in the rear.

The novice Polish Lieutenant trailed McLane like a shadow. In a sudden blurt of breathless words he gasped, "I place my men under your command, Lieutenant."

McLane frowned. "What?"

"You and your soldiers are veterans, yes?"

"Yes."

"I am not," Lieutenant Lewandowski confessed. "I have not… not seen action. My men are raw recruits… so I place myself and my soldiers under your command."

McLane didn't have time to do anything other than react. He was a natural-born leader. He pointed to the Wolverines. "Okay. The first thing I want you to do is move those three APCs off the road. They're not going to stop a Russian tank, so I want them on the shoulder of the highway," he pointed to a nearby plateau of level ground studded with trees. "From there they will be able to cover the farm fields along the riverbank. If the Russians try to land paratroopers to attack the bridge, your APCs will be in position to stop them dead. Understand?"

The Polish Lieutenant nodded his head enthusiastically and dashed towards the bridge with his hands cupped to his mouth, screaming orders to the crews of the armored personnel carriers. One by one the eight-wheeled Wolverines rolled off the road and into their new positions, their wicked Bushmaster cannons trained to overlook the vulnerable open ground to the west.

"Now get your crews to throw up whatever earthworks they can muster; rocks, earth, fallen tree trunks – anything that will give the APCs some cover against Russian RPG fire."

The Polish crews went to work with a will, driven on by their Lieutenant while McLane went in search of Sergeant Block. He found the man on the opposite side of the highway, deep inside the fringe of trees. Barnsley's Challenger 2 had been reversed into a hull-down position behind an uprooted tree with a clear line of fire straight down the highway. Block was at the bottom of a waist-deep trench, covered in dirt and with a trenching tool in his big hands, digging alongside the Polish troops. The trench was located a hundred yards east of the tank, well inside the woods, from where the Polish infantry would be able to defend the tank's flank against Russian infantry with RPGs. Similar entrenchments were being dug to support the other two Challengers further along the road.

McLane peered skywards. The day was darkening, made gloomier by the blanket of black smoke that stained the sky. The forest was filled with deep shadows that would offer the infantry little warning of an enemy attack. He motioned for Sergeant Block to join him.

The Sergeant handed his trenching tool to a young Polish soldier and climbed from the pit dusting dirt from his hands. "The Polish have two Javelin teams attached to their Platoon," McLane said. "But I don't know how good they are. Who is our best man on the one-forty-eight?"

"Gardiner," Sergeant Block didn't need to ponder the question.

"Okay. Give him a Javelin and find positions for the two teams forward of the tanks – but tell them to keep out of the fight until after the Challengers open fire."

Block nodded. "Where do you want the rest of us?"

"The Poles are raw recruits – never fought before. I need you, Mallinson and Scully to nursemaid a trench each and keep them under control."

It was a plan; a hasty plan, but it was all there was time for because just sixty seconds later three Russian BMP-2s suddenly rounded the corner and rumbled into view.

Chapter 8:

The distance between the bend in the road and the southern approach to the Nogat River Bridge was less than a thousand yards. The driver of the leading Russian armored personnel carrier took the turn at thirty miles an hour. The vehicle's commander saw the Polish trucks and four-wheel drives blocking his path and ordered his gunner to open fire.

"Damn!" Lieutenant Barnsley in the turret of his Challenger 2 cursed bitterly as the first Russian machine gun rounds flew wide of the engineers on the bridge. The British officer had been hoping his snare would produce richer initial pickings than just a few enemy APCs. His tank was set back from the road in good leafy cover and behind the trunk of a fallen tree. He knew that once his Troop opened fire the enemy would instantly pinpoint their positions.

"One-One, take the bastards out!" he snapped the order.

Call sign One-One sat hidden in a grove of trees closer to the bend, wedged within a shallow gully of leaf-covered woodlands. The tank had been parked hull-down and angled to the road, giving the Sergeant in command of the vehicle a broadside shot at all three enemy APCs.

The Challenger 2's muzzle flashed a blinding fireball of flame and a split-second later the lead BMP-2 was torn into a thousand steel fragments by the thundering impact of a HESH round that struck flush on the hull. For several seconds the highway became blotted out by a black column of smoke as a roiling fireball of blooming orange flames engulfed the Russian vehicle, continuing to grow upon itself as fragments of twisted metal were flung hundreds of feet into the air. The percussive 'crack!' of the explosion was an ear-splitting hammer blow that beat against the sky.

The second BMP-2 erupted in a lightning strike of flames eight seconds later. The HESH round tore into the heart of the Russian troop carrier and blew it apart from the inside. The turret was torn off the hull by the crushing force of the explosion and flung into the nearby trees trailing a comet of sparks and flames. The entire superstructure above the steel tracks and chassis seemed to disintegrate as billowing smoke engulfed it.

The commander of the third BMP-2 witnessed the savage destruction of the other two vehicles and roared frantically for his driver to reverse. The interior of the Russian troop carrier filled with panicked shouts in the face of imminent death. The driver reversed at high speed, the vehicle weaving across the highway in a futile attempt to throw off the British tank's aim. The Challenger 2's massive main gun roared a third time and the BMP-2 exploded into flames and fragments.

The silence after the roar of gunfire was eerie. A dense cloudbank of smoke drifted over the blacktop and crept through the woods, twisting like tendrils of grey mist.

Lieutenant Barnsley watched the destruction of the enemy APCs with grim professional satisfaction. The devastation had been clinical and complete, and as a consequence, the highway had been turned into an apocalyptic wasteland of fire and smoke and twisted metal wreckage. Black ash swirled in the air and fell from the smoke-stained sky like gentle rain. Spot fires had been sparked on the edge of the woods by burning debris, and the litter-strewn blacktop was stained black with blood and burning fuel.

He popped the commander's hatch and lifted his head. The stench of cordite and diesel fumes pricked at his nostrils. He turned his gaze towards the north and saw the Polish engineers, pale-faced and shaken, still working furiously to prepare the bridge for demolition. He watched them for several seconds and then his attention was distracted by a figure on the opposite side of the highway.

Close to one of the Wolverine APCs, Lieutenant McLane stood paused with his hands on his hips, his head lifted to the sky and his whole body drawn rigid with tension. Barnsley suspiciously lifted his own eyes to the darkening clouds, visible through the canopy of forest trees.

For a long moment the world seemed held in the grips of an eerie stillness, and it was several seconds before a new sound separated itself from the background murmur of ambient battlefield noise and solidified into the beat of spinning helicopter rotors and the shrill whine of turbine engines.

The sound came on, growing louder and clearer every second. Then, suddenly, the thick cloudbanks of dark smoke became wind-whipped into shreds by the violent gusts of a downdraft.

The Russian helicopters appeared overhead preceded by a skirt of shrieking wind and a thundering cacophony of engine roar. There were six of the ungainly beasts, flying low above the treetops and approaching from the south. Lieutenant Barnsley dropped back down inside the steel of his turret and slammed the hatch closed. The Russian helicopters were not his fight but he recognized the ominous danger they represented. For a moment his thoughts drifted to the American Lieutenant. Through the viewing prisms around his cupola, he saw McLane suddenly explode into movement, his hands cupped to his mouth as he shouted a warning and his body animated with urgency.

Barnsley watched the Russian helicopters pass overhead, turning west as they began to sink down the sky. Then all his attention was wrenched back to the bend in the road by an urgent warning from his gunner.

"Enemy armor! T-90's in sight!"

Two dark hulking shapes appeared through the haze.

The two Russian T-90 MBTs nosed cautiously around the highway corner at low speed and took up firing positions on the gravel either side of the blacktop, partially obscured by the fringe of elm trees and scrubland that grew all the way to the tarmac. Tactically the Russians had little choice. The section of highway south of the bridge was formed into a tight funnel by the surrounding forest that gave them no room for armored maneuvers. Their only option was to bludgeon their way through the enemy, relying on speed and savage firepower to overwhelm the defenders. But first the nature and strength of the Allied resistance needed to be discovered – and for that to happen, the lives of Russian tankers had to be gambled. Once the two T-90s were in their overwatch positions, four more camouflaged steel monsters came charging around the bend, running the gauntlet at high speed and popping off smoke canisters as they surged towards the bridge.

"All tanks open fire!" Barnsley barked the order.

One-One and One-Two fired simultaneously. The leading T-90 was struck flush on the hull from a range of just a few hundred yards. The APFSDS long dart penetrator pierced the enemy tank's armor and tore through the driver's compartment. The impact of the direct hit from such close range was cataclysmic. The T-90 was consumed in smoke, and a split-second later overwhelmed by flaring jets of fire that erupted through sprung hatches. The tank's turret blew off as a series of secondary explosions tore the iron beast apart from within, slaughtering the crew. The T-90 rolled on, driverless and out of control, trailing flames and thick black smoke. It veered off the highway and rammed into a tree where it continued to burn like an inferno, setting fire to the fringe of the forest and a swathe of bushland.

The second T-90 suffered an equally catastrophic fate; struck on the side of the turret by One-One as the vehicle passed the British Challenger's concealed position. The range was so close the muzzle flash from the Challenger seemed to join with the Russian tank for an instant before the T-90 was shunted sideways by the ferocity of the armor piercing round. The turret was cleaved clean off the Russian tank and thrown end over end into the nearby trees. A fierce torch of flame erupted from the hull of the decapitated MBT as a thundercloud of dense black smoke spewed from the wreckage. The ruined carcass stopped dead on its tracks in the middle of the highway, blocking one lane and forcing the following two Russian tanks to swerve suddenly.

"Fin tank!" Barnsley waited until one of the trailing enemy MBTs emerged through the curtain of smoke and burst into the open. The Challenger 2 fired and the recoil of the heavy round blasting from the muzzle sent a liquid pulse through the steel hull. The armor piercing round struck the T-90 flush on the front of the turret but incredibly – even at such close range – the enemy tank's Kontakt-5 ERA (explosive reactive armor) and composite compound built into the turret defeated the British munition. The Russian tank seemed to flinch on the road, like a boxer taking a heavy blow, then surged onwards, firing smoke canisters as its turret turned towards Barnsley's Challenger.

"Target go on!" Barnsley hissed. The barrel of the T-90 swung in his direction until it seemed he was staring directly down the yawning black hole of the enemy tank's muzzle.

"Loaded!"

"Firing!" the gunner seated in front of Barnsley snapped.

The view through Barnsley's primary sight was obscured for a heartbeat by the fiery bloom of the tank's muzzle flash as the round sped from the barrel and drove straight through the heart of the Russian tank's hull. The armor piercing dart struck the T-90 on the front left track guard, mangling the steel track and front drive wheel before piercing the hull and disintegrating. The carnage caused by the explosion killed everyone aboard the Russian tank an instant before the interior exploded in flames and smoke.

"Target!"

"Target stop!" Barnsley acknowledged the destruction of the T-90 and immediately began searching for the fourth and final enemy tank that had rounded the bend. He found it amidst the smoke and carnage but it was obscured behind the blazing hulk of one of the other destroyed Russian tanks, turning broadside on the road as if it intended to bulldoze its way into the tree line.

"One-One, take the bastard out before he reaches the woods!"

One-One fired a snap-shot that missed the enemy tank. The T-90 swished its tail to the Challenger and mounted the shoulder of the road, knocking down trees as it desperately sought the refuge of the woods. The gunner in One-One re-lased the target and fired again. The second shot from the Challenger took the enemy tank in the stern and ripped clean through the T-90's flimsy tail armor. The Russian tank seemed to shudder as the APFSDS round punctured its hull. The vehicle blew apart behind a flash of orange light.

The two T-90s on overwatch retaliated with return fire, pinpointing the positions of the three British tanks and aiming through the smoke and flames. Both tanks targeted the closest Challenger, firing a heartbeat apart. The first Russian round exploded on the lip of the gully where One-One was concealed. The impact of the eruption shook the British MBT violently and a hail of thrown earth rained down the tank's hull armor. The second Russian tank fired and missed the Challenger completely.

The Sergeant commanding One-One switched to his TI (thermal-imaging) sights and peered through the billowing grey smoke that engulfed the highway.

"Fin, tank!"

The turret turned to align with the commander's primary sight aiming mark.

"On!" the gunner identified the target and laid his GPS aiming mark on the center mass of the T-90 positioned on the inside bend of the road. The enemy MBT was stationary behind the incline of the sloping ground, effectively giving it hull-down cover from attack.

"Loaded!"

"Firing!" he jammed his thumb down on the trigger.

The thirty-foot muzzle blast leaped from the barrel of the Challenger, flattening the surrounding shrubs. The armor piercing projectile flashed across the sky in the blink of an eye and exploded well wide of its target.

"Christ!" the Sergeant spat his frustration. "Target go on!"

Both tanks fired again, almost simultaneously. The T-90's shot struck the turret of the defiladed Challenger 2, whanging off the thick frontal armor. The toll of the deflected shot rang like a huge bell inside the British tank's hull.

"Firing!"

Again the shot from the British tank flew wide of the enemy tank, disappearing to the stern of the T-90 and exploding in the depths of the forest. One-Two joined the fight, firing from a position closer to the bridge. Shooting from a better angle and with the T-90's hull partially exposed, the second British Challenger scored a hit on the Russian tank's left track, immobilizing the enemy vehicle. Realizing their sudden vulnerability, the three man crew of the T-90 bailed out through the tank's hatches and scrambled into the relative safety of the woods.

With the initial attack devastated, the surviving T-90 on overwatch reversed from cover and withdrew behind the bend in the road, popping off a dozen smoke canisters to conceal its retreat. Lieutenant Barnsley breathed a tight sigh of relief.

"All tanks hold your fire!" he announced. The opening gambit had been fought and the Russian attack stalemated. But to the west, in the fields that bordered the riverbank, the fight to win the bridge was only just beginning.

*

The six Russian helicopters came swooping over the forest treetops in a roar of clattering noise. They flew in line astern formation, barely two hundred feet off the ground. Once over the farm fields to the west of the bridge they circled in the air above the landing zone, bringing their nose-mounted 12.7mm machineguns to bear on the highway. The first of the helicopters dropped down through the smoke quickly. The moment it touched the ground the rear clamshell doors opened and almost two dozen Russian paratroopers spilled out.

From his position atop the treelined rise of ground at the edge of the highway, McLane watched the enemy helicopters with reluctant admiration. The Russians were professional, their tactics straight out of the textbook. He studied the helicopters carefully and was sure they were the same six aircrafts he had seen earlier approaching the bridge at Elblag.

"The Russians mean business," he murmured. The Ml-8TVs (Hip-E) assault helicopters were ungainly and grotesquely shaped, with the rotors mounted over the twin turboshaft engines at the body midsection and external stores bristling from weapons racks on each side of the long bus-like body. The nose of the helicopter was rounded and there were two massive round air intakes directly above the cockpit like huge misshapen eyes. As soon as the lead helicopter had disgorged its cargo of soldiers, it leaped back into the air and banked away to the south, flying low and fast.

The Russian paratroopers were from the elite 45th Detached Reconnaissance Regiment. They fanned out in the featureless muddy field to secure the LZ, weapons aimed towards the rise of ground where the three Polish APCs were concealed. McLane had just a handful of Polish troops and vehicle crewmen with him; he was counting on the Bushmasters mounted in the turrets of the Rosomaks to blunt the force of the Russian assault.

As he watched on, the second Russian Hip-E dropped down out of the sky and settled in the muddy field. Another twenty Russian paratroopers dashed from the cargo bay of the helicopter and sprinted towards the fringe of trees that grew along the riverbank. McLane narrowed his eyes. The Russians were dressed in a miss-match of uniforms; some men wearing the distinctive blue beret of Russian paratroopers, others wearing helmets. Yet other men wore black balaclavas. Their uniforms too were a mottled collection of differing camouflage patterns, yet they moved with the well-coordinated precision of elite veteran troops.

McLane guessed the Russians were delivering a full company of paratroopers to the battlefield. They would be hardened veterans from the fighting in the Baltics and around the Polish capital. He clenched his jaw, fretting over the moment to unleash the Bushmasters. Once he opened fire, he could expect the Russians to retaliate with everything in their arsenal. McLane watched the third Hip-E circle and then drift down the sky for a landing. He was worried about the nose-mounted machine guns each helicopter carried. Whilst ever the Hips were over the battlefield, the Russian infantry had the advantage of overwhelming firepower and brutal air support. But the longer he delayed meant he would have more enemy infantry to deal with.

"I reckon waiting is the right thing to do…" Sergeant Block had appeared at McLane's shoulder. He stared at the Russian paratroopers spilling out of the third Hip-E, watching the way they moved and the speed at which they dispersed from the vulnerable helicopter to find soft cover. "We'll have our hands full with just the infantry, if you ask me."

"What are you doing here?" McLane frowned, his voice irritated although secretly he was grateful for the veteran Sergeant's advice.

"Nothing happening in the woods yet. The Russian tanks are just testing our positions. They'll try to smash their way through with armor again before they bring infantry through the forest to attempt an outflanking maneuver."

McLane grunted. Down by the river the fourth and fifth Hip-Es were hovering over the farm field, coming in to land. The ground had been churned to a muddy bog by the trampling boots of the paratroopers. McLane estimated there were around a hundred enemy soldiers spread out between the edge of the riverbank and a low wire fence two hundred yards to the south.

McLane looked up into the darkening sky. The setting sun was smothered by banks of smoke, turning the end of day into a weak watery twilight. Then he looked to the bridge. The engineers were becoming difficult to see in the shadows of the tall woods.

"Thirty minutes until sunset?"

Block glanced at his watch. "Thirty five."

"I hope those fucking engineers know their job…" he left the words hanging. If the demolition of the bridge failed then this fight would have all been for nothing.

"I hope they can tell time," Sergeant Block growled. "We ain't gonna be able to hold the Ruskies back for long."

McLane walked to the nearest Wolverine. The APC was parked broadside to the farm field under the cover of several tall bushy trees, its hull partially concealed by a crude low wall of stone and earth. The vehicle's gunner had his head out of the turret, watching the Russian infantry in the field with huge fear-filled eyes.

"Wait for my signal before you open fire," McLane kept his voice confident as he went between the three vehicles, issuing the same order. The Polish Lieutenant joined Block and McLane. He was breathless, twitching with fear and anxiety. His eyes were huge as saucers. Over their shoulder the final Hip-E touched down. It landed closer to the riverbank and spent a full sixty seconds on the ground while men carrying crates of equipment were unloaded. Finally the sound of the helicopter's twin turbines rose to a shrieking whine and the ungainly beast lifted once more into the sky, clattering away to the south in pursuit of the other gunships.

McLane watched the disappearing Hip-E until it was just a distant dark speck against the twilight sky and then at last turned his attention to the defense of the bridge. The handful of Polish infantry around him were laying prone along the crest of the rising ground, concealed in long grass. One of them fiddled nervously with the weapon in his hands. Another crossed himself and mouthed a silent prayer to his God. From somewhere down in the farm field a shrill whistle sounded and the paratroopers slowly rose to their feet.

The waiting was over.

The Russians were coming.

*

The paratroopers moved in short, rapid bounds, rising to their feet, sprinting forward, and then throwing themselves down in the mud to cover the advance of the group following behind them. They were well-drilled, coming closer with menacing silence. There were no cheers, no barked orders from officers. By the riverbank three five-man 82mm mortar teams were set up, and along the edge of the wire fence to the south two-man crews crouched behind heavy machine guns, covering the remorseless advance. The Russians came on determinedly, their movements like some vast choreographed dance. McLane watched them and couldn't help but feel apprehensive admiration.

"They're good," he grudgingly admitted.

"Yeah," Block grunted. "But they can't dodge bullets. Let's see what the fuckers are like under fire."

The closest Russians reached a narrow irrigation ditch five hundred yards short of the highway and still the menacing silence persisted, drawing taut the nerves of every man who knew that any moment hell would be unleashed. The Polish Lieutenant too was fidgeting in agitation. He glanced sideways at McLane who shook his head.

"No. Wait…"

Suddenly a sound like a deep cough echoed across the tense silence and from out of the trees along the riverbank a mortar shell arced into the sky. It landed at the foot of the gentle rise and exploded in a billow of thick white smoke. There was a short pause and then all three Russian 2B24 mortars fired in unison. The rounds landed amongst the trees where the Polish APCs were concealed. The explosions sent a ripple of startled panic through the raw Polish troops. McLane grimaced. He had hoped to hold fire until the enemy were closer and kills could be guaranteed. Now the element of smoke had unraveled his plan.

McLane turned. The engineers were reversing one of the trucks off the bridge. He turned back to see the nearest Russians wading across the knee-high water of the irrigation ditch. The enemy had begun to lose some of their rigid cohesion now the highway was so close. They began to hurry; to lengthen their strides. Some paratroopers began to wonder if the bridge was defended with Allied infantry at all. Others knew damned well that they were running into a hailstorm of resistance. They were eager to get the initial shock of combat over. They gritted their teeth, grunted with the effort of dashing across the muddy ground, and braced themselves for the first inevitable Allied fusillade.

McLane looked to the young Polish Lieutenant. The closest paratroopers were less than four hundred yards from the rise of ground. "Fire!"

The Polish officer gave the signal and the three Bushmaster machine guns mounted in the turrets of the TKO Rosomak APCs roared to life, spitting savage fury down the incline.

McLane drew his M4 to his shoulder and added his firepower to the opening fusillade. The weapon kicked in his grip as he squeezed the trigger, aiming for a paratrooper who had just cleared the obstacle of the drainage ditch. He missed; the Russian ran on, then threw himself down in the mud and fired back.

To McLane's dismay the Russians seemed unwavering in their advance. He could see three or four enemy soldiers were down in the mud, but the rest ran on untouched. He spun round and studied the leaping tongues of fire flickering from the muzzles of the Bushmasters.

"Aim lower!" McLane shouted. It was pointless. The sound of his voice was swamped by the ripping roar of the 30mm chain gun. He sprang to his feet, livid with outrage and charged towards the nearest APC. "You're firing too fuckin' high! Cut them off at the knees!" he roared.

Typical of inexperienced troops, the Polish were shooting high, not allowing for the incline of the slope affecting the accuracy of their aim. The first fusillade that he had hoped would set the Russians back on their heels and decimate their number had been utterly wasted. Now the advantage of surprise was gone.

McLane cursed.

"Aim for their balls!" he dashed amongst the small line of Polish infantry laying in the long grass forward of the armored personnel carriers. He went to each man, repeating the message, "Aim low! Aim low!"

The Russians went to ground as the opening Allied salvo plucked at the smoke-swirling air above them. From the southern flank of the field the Russian heavy machine gun opened fire on the ridgeline, suppressing the Polish infantry.

The paratroopers gathered themselves and sprang to their feet. *"Ataka!"* a huge bellowing voice amidst their ranks roared, and the sheer volume and energy of the cried order seemed to propel the paratroopers forward. *"Zakhvatit' most!* Seize the bridge!"

A tide of paratroopers reached the foot of the slope in a ragged wave. One of the Russians fired up the incline and a Polish infantryman cried out in bloody agony.

The enemy mortars joined the fight, firing HE rounds over the heads of their advancing troops and peppering the crest of the rise. Two shells overshot their mark by several yards and exploded on the highway, but the third landed close by one of the Rosomaks, rocking the vehicle on its suspension and peppering the steel hull with fragments. Another Polish infantryman went down, clawing at his eyes and screaming in excruciating agony. There was blood on his hands. He fell into the long grass, sobbing.

The flood of paratroopers started pounding up the grassy slope. Sergeant Block watched them come on. He saw an officer, saw the blue beret. The man was wearing a camouflage jacket, open to the waist, with a Major's star on the epaulets. Block snatched up his M4 and fired a short spray of automatic fire. Two Russian paratroopers went down screaming. One soldier was shot in the face. The man's head snapped back and a tinge of pink mist hung in the air. He fell backwards and his corpse rolled to the bottom of the slope. The second man sagged forward clutching his torso and vomited blood into the grass. The Russian Major who had been beside the men ran on, untouched.

"Fire!" McLane shouted.

The handful of Polish infantry laying prone in the long grass took aim on the closest wave of Russian paratroopers and blazed away with their automatic weapons. It was a spray of panic fire, lacking discipline – but the results at such short range were murderous. As many as twenty enemy paratroopers went down in the fusillade. One enemy soldier had both legs shot from underneath him and fell screaming in the mud. Another man was shot in the groin and cried out, appalled by the gruesome wound. He clutched his hands over the bleeding injury and gasped for breath, then fell sideways, tucking his knees to his chest as the waves of agony washed over him and the blood soaked his trousers.

The three gunners in the turrets of the Rosomak Wolverine APCs switched to their coaxial machine guns and added their throaty roar to the thunder of gunfire. The Russian attack up the rise began to waver. Men screamed. One paratrooper dropped to his knees, blinded by gushing blood from a head wound. His comrades ran past him. Others were writhing in the mud, clutching at gaping wounds or sobbing softly. But still the elite Russians advanced.

They sensed how fragile and small the Allied force ahead of them was and their pride goaded them on to glory. They cried a snarling challenge as they charged again into the waiting guns, driven on by their officers and their fearless courage. They were the Russian Army's elite; veterans of the Chechen wars, the South Ossetia War, the Ukraine Intervention and the savage fight for Warsaw.

"Fire!"

Another handful of paratroopers fell bleeding to the guns. One Russian dropped into the grass near the crest of the rise and lobbed a grenade into the tree line. The explosion killed three Polish infantrymen; heaved them bodily into the air and eviscerated them as the ground erupted in an exploding flash of flame. The Polish Lieutenant reeled away clutching at his arm and gasping in pain, struck by shrapnel fragments. He staggered against the hull of the nearest Wolverine his arm hanging uselessly by his side and awash with blood. "Keep firing!" he screamed bravely, but it sounded more like a sob.

McLane sensed the battle hung on a knife-edge. The momentum of the Russian attack had been broken on the barrels of the Rosomaks coaxial machine guns. It would take only one more concerted effort to push the enemy back down the slope in retreat. But the handful of Polish infantry who clung desperately to the ridgeline had taken heavy casualties too. He looked around in desperation, seeking a wild solution and his eyes fastened on the closest Wolverine. He ran.

The wounded Polish Lieutenant saw McLane approaching. "Can you still fight?" McLane asked. He noticed the Lieutenant's blood-soaked sleeve.

"Yes." The young man nodded bravely. He was pale-faced.

"Good, then you can drive. Get behind the wheel of this thing and charge the bastards."

"Lieutenant?" the Polish officer gaped.

"You heard me. I want you to charge down the slope, machine gun blazing and rout them."

The Lieutenant nodded manfully and climbed aboard the Wolverine. The engine rumbled to life and the Lieutenant reversed back to clear a stand of trees, then the vehicle surged forward, its eight wheels jouncing over broken ground until it swung to face the slope and leaped forward, bustling down the gradual incline and into the ragged remains of the enemy with the gunner in the turret sawing the coax machine gun from side to side.

The paratroopers broke.

Under the lashing fury of machine gun fire and the sudden charge of the APC, they stumbled backwards then turned and ran. The Wolverine came under fire from the Russian heavy machine gun and shot back. The Russian team were in soft cover behind a fold of ground near the field's wire perimeter defense. A solid hail of lead cut them to pieces.

McLane watched the slaughter from the top of the rise with grim satisfaction. The company of paratroopers had been decimated and the Russian attack broken. The Wolverine swerved back across the ploughed field, cutting down stragglers. Then a darting white streak of light flashed across the sky, fired from a grove of trees by the riverbank. The Polish Lieutenant saw the flash of light from the corner of his eye and knew with fatal certainty that it was death approaching.

The RPG missile had been fired by one of the Russian heavy weapons team manning the mortars. The missile flew like a dart on a wobbling tail of white smoke and struck the armored personnel carrier broadside. The impact of the savage explosion blew the Wolverine apart; consumed it in a fireball of smoke and flames and twisted metal fragments. The wicked *'crack!'* of the missile exploding echoed across the sky.

McLane stared on in horror, watching the black column of smoke rising into the twilight sky. The lurid bonfire of flames were bright flickering tongues of orange that cast a hellish glow.

The fight to hold the bridge had come at a terrible cost, and still the battle was not yet over. From the far side of the highway and from somewhere deep within the woods came the sudden sound of automatic weapons fire. Sergeant Block and McLane exchanged ominous glances. The Russians were in the woods and attempting to outflank the British tank positions.

Chapter 9:

Sergeant Block turned on his heel, his face ashen, and sprinted across the highway, into the dense palisade of woodlands where two of the British Challengers were concealed.

He ran with his arms pumping, driven by desperation and despair. His combat kit and spare ammunition magazines flapped about his waist, and his body armor felt like a lead weight across his chest.

He dashed past Lieutenant Barnsley's tank, over the uneven leaf-covered ground, his arm waving, voice bellowing. "Scully! Scully!"

He pounded up a gentle incline then down the other side into the shadow-struck gloom of a narrow gulch. With relief he saw the semi-circle of dug trenches still manned. He dropped down into a waist-deep pit beside Corporal Jane Scully and sucked in three deep lungsful of ragged breath.

"Where are the bastards? How many? Have you taken casualties?"

Scully pointed further to the south east, deeper into the darkening woods. "Mallinson has the section protecting One-Two's position. There was a firefight thirty seconds go. The Russians came in numbers but I think Mallinson's Polish recruits drove them back. Since then it's been quiet, like they're building up to something."

Block narrowed his eyes and peered into the dappled undergrowth. He knew exactly where Mallinson's section were positioned because he had sighted the trenches himself. They were about a hundred yards further south, arranged in a protective semi-circle around the exposed flank of the second Challenger; tank One-Two. He squinted into the fading light and thought he saw movement. Each network of trenches was connected by Polish hand-held section radios. He keyed the mike and crouched down low in the pit, keeping his voice to a rumbling murmur.

"Mallinson? Report in."

"We're here, Sarge," Mallinson's voice sounded reedy and shaken with whispered strain. "The Russians are to our east. We had a brief contact. No one injured."

Block let out the breath he had been holding. "Roger that. Out."

The two nests of American and Polish troops crouched in uneasy silence for several minutes. All of Sergeant Block's senses were attuned to the vague haunting sounds that came from deeper in the woods. His instincts told him that the enemy were there – somewhere in the gloom – waiting to attack. He glanced at his watch and winced; another fifteen minutes until he could anticipate the green flare from the bridge. It was a long time to hold off a determined enemy.

The Russian attack began behind a salvo of 82mm mortar fire that arced high into the sky and plunged down through the forest canopy. The first rounds were high explosive; they landed in the undergrowth around the trenches and burst apart with a muffled *'crump!'* that threw debris and fallen foliage into the air. Trees shook and leaves rained down. Branches splintered and fell crashing to the ground. The Polish recruits sank down in the bottom of their pits and cringed as the world above them whipped and cracked with shrapnel fragments.

The Russian mortar teams switched to smoke and blanketed the forest's fringe with a white twisting veil that cut visibility to less than a hundred yards.

Then they charged.

The attack spread across the rim of the woods and came borne on a roar of ragged shouts and spattering small arms fire. Russian infantry dashed out of the haze, dropped to their knees amongst the trees, and opened fire. The Polish infantry shot back. Block saw a Russian rise to his feet, preparing to dash towards fresh cover. A round from a Polish rifle caught the enemy soldier high on the thigh. He clutched at the wound and dropped his weapon, then staggered backwards and fell screaming to the ground.

"Make each shot count!" Block raised his voice above the rising spatter of small arms fire, keeping his tone level to steady the Polish recruits. "We hold them here. We have to hold them here so make every shot count."

More Russians appeared on the flank, trying to circle around behind the British tanks and sever their escape route to the bridge. Scully pointed to the mass of shapes, drifting in the shadows. "More of the bastards coming around behind us."

Block turned half the men in the trench to face the new threat. They were hovering in the gloom just beyond effective range. Then a whistle sounded and the mass of enemy soldiers separated from the wall of shadows and came forward, materializing into the solid shapes of running men.

"Fire!" Block barked.

The Polish infantry shot well, but for every Russian that fell, it seemed like another enemy soldier appeared to take their place. They swarmed through the woods, darting between the palisade of trees, pausing sometimes behind cover to shoot before dashing forward again. They broke into small knots, supporting each other as they pushed remorselessly closer to the trenches. The sound of battle rose to a crescendo of snapping whip-cracks of noise that became a continuous hail of horror that slashed through the air.

Block fought as a rifleman, shoulder to shoulder with the Polish. The battlefield seemed to telescope down to a few smoke-streaked feet of forest. More mortar shells exploded and the sounds of men screaming became a gruesome soundtrack to the savagery. He saw a Russian in the trees about a hundred yards away and took careful aim. The enemy soldier leaned out from behind cover and raised his weapon. Block shot the man in the chest and saw him thrown back by the impact. Block ducked down into the bottom of the pit to reload a fresh magazine, and when he rose again to seek more targets, he saw the same Russian he had just shot getting back to his feet. Block swore and fired again, this time hitting the enemy soldier in the shoulder. The man clapped his hand over the wound and swayed out of sight, blood spilling through his fingers.

"Keep firing! Keep firing!" the American Sergeant's voice boomed, even above the rising roar of gunfire. The Polish infantryman next to him was dead, shot in the face, and there were two more Polish soldiers laying in the bottom of the trench, unmoving and blood-spattered.

"Keep firing!"

More Russians continued to appear from out of the deepening shadows of the forest to reinforce those already swarming forward. An enemy infantryman wielding a PK machine gun found a rise of ground on the left flank of the attack and opened fire, spraying the trench line with fresh death. A Polish infantryman screamed in terror and dropped to the bottom of the pit sobbing pitifully as a furious thunder of bullets stitched the soil just inches from his head. "Christ!" Block snarled. All he could see of the enemy machine gun position was the wicked flickering muzzle flash. "We can't last much longer!"

He snatched for the radio and shouted. "Mallinson! Mallinson! Report your situation!"

There was a hiss of static across the receiver and then Mallinson's voice came wavering and broken. "Most dead… heavy fire we… pinned down…"

"Mallinson!" Block shook the radio, then threw it aside in frustration. From the lip of the trench, he stared south and saw Mallinson's position overwhelmed and surrounded by grey swarming shapes. Winking lights of muzzle flash still split the gloom, but they were fading, becoming less frenzied. It was a hundred yards, but it might as well have been a million miles. Three dull grenade explosions flashed then faded, and in the aftermath the stuttering gunfire from Mallinson's valiant defiance was abruptly snuffed out.

Block growled impotent outrage and turned his fury on three Russian infantrymen who tried to rush the far end of the trench. He swung his M4 and aimed low, cutting the three men down with a savage swathe of bullets. The enemy soldiers went down screaming. Block pulled a grenade and threw it far out into the killing zone. "Frag out!"

The woods around the trench dissolved into a curtain of erupting dirt. When the dust settled, all three Russians were dead.

In the stunned aftermath of the explosion the forest canopy became lit by a brilliant green light that arced across the sky on a wavering tail of white smoke. It hung in the air for long seconds, casting a glow over the battlefield and bathing the last of the days light in its blindingly bright halo. Block lifted his eyes and peered through the canopy of foliage and recognized the green signal flare. "Time to bug out!" he cried.

At the very same instant two streaking white lights flashed through the dense undergrowth. Block saw them appear out of the gloom and arrow through the trees to the south. He turned his head just in time to see two RPG-29 'Vampir' projectiles strike the hull of Challenger One-Two and detonate.

The shoulder-launched Russian rockets hit the British tank broadside. The first missile destroyed two of the tank's left side road wheels. The second 'Vampir' projectile penetrated the tank's hull, killing all four men inside the tank. The thunderous noise of the explosions and the blinding flash of fire that followed lit the woods up like daylight.

Block swore. He seized Scully by the shoulder and spun her around. "Get these boys outa here! Get them back to the bridge."

He shoved Scully towards the far end of the trench and reloaded his M4. "I'll cover you until you reach the highway."

Scully waited for the flames from the burning Challenger to fade, then leaped from the trench and ran doubled-over towards the fringe of the forest. There were just four Polish survivors. They ran in her shadow, frightened and frantic. They reached Lieutenant Barnsley's Challenger and took temporary shelter behind the vehicle's massive steel bulk. The tank began reversing, its steel tracks churning the soft forest undergrowth, adding the deafening whine of its massive powerpack to the chaos and clamor of the battlefield.

Scully broke from the fringe of trees and ran out onto the highway. She saw Lieutenant McLane standing near the bridge. The last of the Polish trucks and four-wheel drives were being driven to the far side of the crossing, clearing the site for imminent demolition. The handful of Polish troops that had defended the shoulder of the road against the Russian paratroopers and the two surviving APCs were emerging from the opposite side of the blacktop. McLane stood waving his arm, urging the vehicles and wounded to hurry to the northern side of the river.

McLane saw Scully and his expression turned from anxiety to dismay. "Where are the rest of the Polish? Where is Mallinson and Sergeant Block?"

"There are no more survivors," Scully rasped. "Mallinson and his squad were overrun by the Russians. They're all dead. One of the Challengers was destroyed by RPGs and Sergeant Block is still in the forest."

"On his own?" McLane was appalled.

"He stayed to cover our exfil."

McLane swore foully, then started running for the trees.

Lieutenant Barnsley's Challenger 2 reversed through the undergrowth, flattening saplings and bushes as it burst onto the highway in a billowing cloud of dust and smoke and scattered debris. The driver straightened the steel beast. Barnsley kept the turret facing south towards the smoke-shrouded bend in the road as the driver began to reverse across the bridge.

"One-one, get the hell out of there!" Barnsley's voice across the Troop net was tense with rising strain. "We're withdrawing across the bridge. Move it!"

For a moment the radio burst into a loud hiss of static and then the voice of the Sergeant commanding Call sign One-one came wavering through the interference.

"Roger Zero-one. Falling back to the bridge."

Russian command sensed the significance of the green signal flare. Two T-90 tanks came swarming around the highway bend with a Platoon of infantry flanking them on foot. The Russians caught the British Sergeant's Challenger just as the tank began extricating itself from its hull-down position within the folds of a shallow gully. In the darkening gloom of dusk, the night sky suddenly lit up with savage flaming flashes and booming thunderclaps of noise as both Russian tanks fired on the hapless Challenger from close range.

The first round struck the British MBT flush on the turret and whanged away harmlessly into the darkening woods. A second round struck the tank's lower frontal armor. The Challenger 2 was utterly defenseless. The Russian armor-piercing round smashed through the tank's exposed hull and the Challenger 2 erupted in a monstrous fireball of flames and boiling black smoke. A fiery inferno leapt a hundred feet into the air and falling shrapnel set nearby trees ablaze. Mercifully, the billowing smoke swallowed everything, draping a heavy black shroud over the dead tank.

Lieutenant Barnsley watched the Challenger's gruesome death from the turret of his tank on the northern side of the bridge. The profound sense of devastation came from far away, seeming to roar and rush in his head as his vision misted. He stared aghast at the black boiling smoke, and when he closed his eyes, the flash of the explosion was still there, seared upon his memory.

"My God," he breathed, and then again, his voice numbed with despair, "my God."

*

McLane ran as fast as his legs would carry him blundering through the woods. The forest was near dark and filled with deep shadows so he ran to the sounds of gunfire and the occasional lurid orange tongues of muzzle flash. The tree line around him seemed to be moving; dark shapes in motion on the edge of his vision. He stumbled over a knotted gnarled root of undergrowth and fell headlong to the ground. He scrambled to his feet, bleeding from cuts and scratches, and ran on. A sudden leaping dragon's breath of flame lit up the gloom, and in the glow of its flare he saw the silhouette of Sergeant Block.

He ducked low. Enemy gunfire whizzed and zinged in the air around him. He reached the edge of the trench gasping, his chest on fire. He threw himself down, panting, in the grass.

"What the fuck are you doing?" he croaked down at his Sergeant standing in the bottom of the trench. "We're pulling the fuck out. C'mon!"

"I ain't going," Sergeant Block's teeth were gritted, his jaw clenched tight. He stood with his back to McLane; facing and firing into the forest with his legs braced and his M4 up to his shoulder. McLane could see dark mud stains on the Sergeant's face and neck.

"What the fuck are you talking about?"

"I ain't going!" Sergeant Block said again, then fired at the dark fleeting shape of a Russian soldier who had appeared from behind a nearby tree. A swathe of bullets cut the man down. He rolled back into the shadows, screaming in agony.

Block snarled vengeful satisfaction then slowly turned and in the fading flickering light. McLane saw the dark spatters on Block's face and neck were blood. "I've been shot," the Sergeant said. "I ain't going anywhere."

Block had taken a bullet high in the chest, above the protective rim of his body armor. The enemy round had shattered his sternum. His combat shirt was awash with blood, his face pale and gaunt. His breath gargled in his throat. The two soldiers exchanged glances and understanding flashed between them. Sergeant Block's face twisted into an ironic grimace. "I guess I picked a shitty little hell hole to die in."

McLane could not hold the man's eyes or find the words to reply. Sergeant Block lowered his weapon for a moment and extended his blood-sticky hand. "Goodbye, Lieutenant McLane."

McLane took Block's hand and stared into the Sergeant's eyes. He saw no fear, only regret tinged with sadness.

"Goodbye, Hank," McLane used the man's first name, his voice muted and hushed by the sorrow of the moment. "Thank you – for everything – for every sacrifice you made and for every time you saved my ass."

Block grunted, then winced as a wave of fresh agony washed over him. "I'll buy you as much time as I can."

*

As the last of the day's light faded and the forest turned dark, the Russian infantry infesting the woods surged forward to overwhelm Sergeant Block's entrenched position. They came as a wave of bodies, dispersed amongst the trees, firing from the hip as they charged. One soldier thew a grenade that landed short of the trench. The ground erupted in flames and heaved dirt. Sergeant Block fired through the drifting dust and an enemy soldier grunted then staggered backwards, a wound in his left arm gushing blood.

Another Russian reached the lip of the trench and fired wildly. Block was so close to the man he could see his disfigured face. The enemy soldier's cheek had been slashed, and a flap of bleeding flesh hung loose to his jaw. Block swung the M4 instinctively and fired from point-blank range. The flurry of bullets struck the enemy soldier under the chin and the impact snatched him back as if he had been pulled by an invisible string. Another Russian fired blindly into the trench from out of the shadows, hitting Block in the thigh. His leg collapsed from beneath him, and he went down in the dirt on one knee, awash with fresh blood.

He raised the M4 and held his finger down on the trigger. The weapon roared and for two seconds the darkness was lit up by a flickering flame of muzzle flash and a juddering roar of valiant resistance.

Then the magazine emptied and the gun fell silent.

Sergeant Block sagged to his knees, his chin still lifted in a final act of defiance, his face splashed with blood, gaping wounds in his chest and leg. A Russian soldier appeared on the edge of the trench and Block suddenly saw the pit for what it would become; his grave.

The enemy soldier peered down into the dark hole and a malicious smile tugged at the corner of his lip. He raised his AK-74 and fired once, shooting Block low in the stomach.

The bullet slammed Sergeant Block down on the ground, punching him onto his back. White hot pain shot through his stomach; a sensation like molten liquid burned through his veins. He lay, still lucid and breathing shallowly, staring up into the dark treetops. He saw the sneering face of the man who shot him. The soldier raised his weapon to fire again but a Russian officer appeared and leaned over the dark opening.

"On uzhe mertv," the officer said. "He's dead already."

The Russians moved off towards the bridge at a run.

Block lay staring up at the night sky. He could hear the shallow gurgle of his breath and feel the throbbing pulses of pain as they crashed through his body. His eyes misted and his vision blurred. He had never married; the Army was his life, so as he lay there with the lifeblood seeping from him, his mind filled with memories of the soldiers he had served with; the band of brothers he had fought alongside in Afghanistan, and then the heroic young men who had died in the bomb-ravaged streets of Paslek.

"I'm coming home," he muttered as the reality of his imminent death overwhelmed him. His vision began to darken and he felt a sudden lift of relief. He began reciting words from the 23rd Psalm before the earth suddenly heaved violently and the flashing thunder of the bridge being demolished ripped through the night.

Sergeant Block smiled one final triumphant time before the darkness closed around him. His expression froze and his stillness became eternal.

*

The pathetic, battle-ravaged convoy of surviving vehicles crept north, keeping open intervals in the darkness to avoid collision, and crawling forward at slow speed. Lieutenant Barnsley's Challenger 2 was in the vanguard, followed by the two remaining KTO Rosomak APCs and a Polish Army four-wheel drive.

The handful of exhausted Polish soldiers and engineers who had survived the fight for the bridge were spread between the armored personnel carriers. McLane, Corporal Scully and Private Gardiner trailed in the four-wheel drive.

Scully, hunched behind the wheel of the tail vehicle, had discarded her body armor and sat in her sweat-stained and blood-spattered combat shirt. The garment clung to her like a damp rag. Every few seconds she glanced up from the road and peered into the rearview mirror.

McLane sat sagged in the back of the vehicle atop a pile of cast-off equipment, weapons, helmets and ammunition. He was wedged in the corner, his head nodding forward to his chest as the vehicle bounced and swayed. Scully drove in bleak silence; a heavy pall of despair and grief draped over the vehicle. Without Sergeant Block's larger-than-life presence, the four-wheel drive seemed bereaved.

Despite the chill night air through the open window, Private Gardiner was sweating. Rivulets of it trickled down his cheeks and clung to the dark unshaven stubble across his chin and jaw. He lit a cigarette, offered one to Scully with shaky fingers, and inhaled deeply. His lower lip trembled. Every few minutes he shivered uncontrollably with the aftershocks of his terror.

Ahead of the four-wheel drive, the road ran due west into the night. Tail lights in the APC's flashed and the vehicles slowed, then pulled on to a dirt side road. Scully touched the brakes and followed. A thin cloud of dust rose in a feathery plume like smoke from a shell burst.

"Lieutenant?" Scully called. "We've stopped."

McLane woke with a bleary-eyed start and peered into the darkness at the gloomy shape of a farm house. He roused himself and climbed stiffly from the vehicle. The Challenger and the two APCs were parked next to the abandoned building.

"We're staying here until dawn," Lieutenant Barnsley declared, but there was no energy in his voice. The words in his mouth had a sorrowful underlying timbre to them. He stood rigid, supervising the unloading of the Rosomaks and there was a wall within him, holding back his grief.

McLane and the British officer walked away from the farm house. Neither man spoke until the vehicles were unloaded and the survivors were inside. McLane stood, steady as a slab of granite, but masking his own deep sorrow. It was something the two men shared, but neither could speak about.

"It's too dangerous to be on the road at night," the British Lieutenant said stiffly to justify the decision to make camp for the night. His eyes were underscored with dark bruises.

McLane nodded. "It will take the Russians at least twelve hours to bring up bridging equipment. I think we're safe until morning. God knows we can do with a few hours' sleep."

They said no more, bearing the burden of their mourning in stoic silence, both fearful that their grief would rise to the surface and betray their brittle façades. When they entered the farm house, the survivors of the battle were strewn across the floor, passed out with exhaustion.

*

McLane woke at dawn to a dreadful sense of foreboding. He lay unmoving for a heartbeat, listening intently to the sounds of the new day. Somewhere far away he thought he heard the muted rumble of artillery. The wind was blowing from the north, muting the sound of the barrage. He shivered. A few gentle drops of rain spattered on the roof. He rose, stiff and aching, and instinctively patrolled the farm house, peering through each window for signs of danger.

"Can you hear the rumble?" Lieutenant Barnsley was in one of the bedrooms with the curtains twitched aside. The morning had dawned cold and bleak, the sky the color of old bruises. The British officer looked haggard; lines chiseled into the corners of his mouth. The definition of his features had been eroded by strain and tragedy so that he looked far older than his years.

"Yeah, I hear it. Artillery?" McLane offered.

"Maybe…" Barnsley was not convinced. "But it's coming from the south west. What would the Russians be bombarding? We're the last Allied troops between here and Gdansk."

They went outside into the cold morning with a rising sense of unease. Barnsley took a pair of binoculars. He climbed up onto the hull of the Challenger from the front, using the tank's bollard hooks, then clambered onto the turret. He put the binoculars to his eyes and peered south.

The farm house had been built on a gentle rise, surrounded by miles and miles of flat, featureless farmland. Some of the fields were freshly sewn with crops, others were ploughed earth. For a long time he stood unmoving staring along the horizon line that crouched below a brooding storm-filled sky. When he lowered the glasses, Barnsley's expression was fixed and under tight control, but the tone of his voice sounded pitifully sad and abandoned.

"It's Russian armor," he said. "They're five or six miles to the south west, heading this way. At least a dozen MBT's – probably T-90s."

"Christ!" McLane swore. "How could the Russians have bridged the Nogat so quickly?"

"I don't think they did," Barnsley climbed wearily down from the tank. "I think they're the vanguard of the force moving towards Gdansk from our west. My guess is the two columns are linking up before they push on to the coast."

Barnsley offered McLane the glasses but the American officer shook his head.

"Can we outrun them?"

Barnsley smiled wanly. "Probably not for long…"

McLane went through the farm house, kicking sleeping soldiers and bellowing at the top of his voice. "Everybody up! Move it! Move it! We're breaking camp in five minutes." In contrast, Lieutenant Barnsley seemed withdrawn and introspective. He took a clean tunic from a carry bag and then pulled out a black Regimental beret. He set it on his head with the silver badge over his left eye, then pulled the brim down towards his right eye until it sat at a dashing angle. He smiled like a man about to embark on a long journey. "I always try to look good for a battle," he said thinly. "The beret isn't supposed to be worn in combat, of course, but I think we can make an exception this morning…"

"What are you talking about?" McLane felt a creeping sense of unease.

"My crew and I are staying," Barnsley said flatly. "You'll take the survivors in the Rosomaks and push on for Gdansk. We'll hold the farm house for as long as we can. That will buy you all the time you need to escape the Russian net and reach safety."

"No," McLane shook his head although his instincts told him there was no other viable option.

"Look," Barnsley leaned close and lowered his voice. "Someone has got to reach Gdansk. Otherwise, every life that has been sacrificed will have been in vain. It's your duty to get these people to safety."

"Christ," McLane reeled away, his expression tortured. Lieutenant Barnsley held out the street map. In the margin he had scribbled an address.

"I have a sister. She lives in Coventry. If you get evacuated back to England…, can you visit her? Tell her I died bravely," he gave a small self-depreciating smile. "And that it was painless…"

McLane took the map. Barnsley seemed relieved. He held out his hand.

"No," McLane backed away. The last man he had shaken hands with was Sergeant Block, now dead in a pit. "No," he said again. "I'll see you in Gdansk."

Barnsley narrowed his eyes, seemed to understand, then nodded his head slowly in agreement of the lie.

Gardiner, Scully and the Polish troops scrambled into the two Rosomak armored personnel carriers. Scully drove the lead vehicle with McLane in the passenger seat. The vehicles took off at high speed, leaving a trail of rising dust in their wake. A kilometer further west the road turned to the north and the farm house disappeared from sight.

Four minutes later they heard the first muffled *'crump!'* of a tank firing. McLane ordered the Rosomaks to the shoulder of the road. He stood on the gravel verge and listened intently. Beyond a stand of trees to the south a column of black smoke rose into the morning sky. Ten seconds later there came another booming retort, followed by a fresh pyre of black oily haze.

"Give 'em hell!" McLane muttered darkly to himself. He could imagine the Challenger 2, hull down and hidden behind a wall of the farm house, firing at the enemy tanks as they encircled the lone British defender, their guns barking like savage dogs around a trapped prey.

He turned back for the open door of the APC. On the brittle silence suddenly came a different sound; a louder explosion, the crack of it echoing against the low dark clouds like a clap of thunder. McLane stiffened.

"What was that?" Scully too recognized the different tenor of the explosion.

"That," McLane said desolately, "was the moment four heroic warriors sacrificed their lives for us."

Chapter 10:

Gdansk was a city under siege.

For days the Russian Air Force had been flying bombing missions over the sprawling metropolis and fighting for control of the skies against Allied jets that were forced to fly patrols from bases in Sweden and Germany to maintain a shroud of protection over the beleaguered port.

On the ground, the streets and the critical buildings within the harbor district were a bomb-ruined shambles. Most of the inhabitants of the city had fled south west to Germany or boarded small commercial vessels to cross the Baltic Sea. In their place were almost one hundred and fifty thousand Allied soldiers; the shattered milling remnants of the troops who had retreated north after the fall of Warsaw.

The soldiers were a ragged rabble. They were British regular infantry, Polish mechanized troops, Canadian paratroopers, French airborne troops, and American light infantry. They were a bedraggled and beaten remanence, exhausted and starving, unkempt and on the verge of annihilation. There were also Allied armored units thrown into the melting pot of tension; American Abrams, some British Challenger 2s and entire squadrons of Polish PT-91 Twardy MBTs, as well as squadrons of American Strykers, two Battalions of British Warrior AFVs, and a smattering of Polish KTO Rosomaks and French VAB VTT armored personnel carriers. There were trucks of every conceivable make and type and phalanxes of light vehicles. There were mobile artillery units and American towed artillery pieces – all crammed together in a city that was being strangled to death by the tightening steel fist of Russian's victorious Armies.

The trapped Allied forces became growingly desperate as the Russians closed the noose around Gdansk. A fleet of Allied military transport vessels gathered off the Polish coast to evacuate the troops but Russian submarines in the Baltic took a terrible toll. Swarms of MiG-29 fighters carrying Kh-31A anti-ship missiles beneath their wings swooped down out of the clouds and attacked the flotilla. The Russian planes were met in the air by Swedish Saab JAS Gripen multirole fighters and Polish F-16s flying from temporary bases in eastern Germany. The grey brooding sky over the Baltic became criss-crossed with streaking missiles as the pilots dueled to the death.

Russian heavy artillery bombarded the outlying suburbs of Gdansk and the small towns scattered to the south. The towns of Straszyn and Pruszcz Gdanski were reduced to rubble as the Russians closed from the east and the south on every road until the skyline encircling the port city seemed to glow and pulse with the flash of distant fire and the muffled rumble of explosions.

The two Rosomaks arrived on the south eastern outskirts of Gdansk at mid-morning and were intercepted by three separate roadblocks, each one manned by nervous Allied soldiers. Finally the vehicles reached the heart of the city and McLane found an American command post on Kowalska Street. It was a shaded narrow laneway lined on both sides by four-story red-brick apartment units. Most of the tall buildings had been devastated by Russian air attacks. There was a couple of Humvees parked by the side of the road amongst the rubble.

The Americans climbed down from the Rosomaks and the Polish infantry drove off in search of their own command post. McLane went up a half-dozen steps and into a ground floor unit with his helmet in one hand and his M4 in the other. He was grey with dust and streaked with sweat and grime. His eyes were red-raw, his face haggard. The room was bare of decoration apart from an American flag that hung on the far wall. In front of the flag was a bank of waist-high desks and around the walls were a motley collection of mis-matched chairs so that it resembled a waiting room. There were a dozen soldiers slumped indolently in seats, their sleeve badges from a handful of different units. McLane strode to the desk. He felt numb with exhaustion, hunger and thirst.

The Adjutant behind the counter frowned. He was a young man with a thin-lipped mouth and sallow cheeks, pock-marked by teenage acne.

"Who are you?" he eyed McLane disdainfully, his expression turning to irritation.

"Lieutenant Simon McLane, 1st Platoon, Charlie Company, 2nd Battalion, 87th Infantry Regiment, 2nd Brigade Combat Team, 10th Mountain Division. I'm looking for my Battalion."

"McLane?" the administrative assistant asked for the spelling and then turned to a laptop and typed the details in with two fingers. After a moment the man frowned and insisted McLane repeat his unit details.

Finally, the Adjutant made a thin dusty sound of discontent. "You're listed as dead. Reported KIA in Paslek."

"Well, I'm alive, as are Corporal Jane Scully and Private Stuart Gardiner from my Platoon," McLane simmered. "We escaped the town and withdrew north to re-join my Battalion."

The Adjutant's frown deepened and he disappeared behind a closed door for several minutes. When he returned, he steered McLane into another office. The walls were plastered with satellite maps of the city. An officer in his fifties rose from behind a large desk. He wore the cleanly-pressed uniform of a US Army Colonel. He had thinning grey hair and the bumptious self-important mannerisms of an accountant.

"I'm Travis," he said gruffly. "Liaison to NATO Command. Your Battalion isn't in Gdansk," he delivered the blunt news. "The entire 87th Infantry Regiment were evacuated to northern Germany by transport ships last night. I'm afraid you're stranded here."

McLane said nothing. He felt suddenly adrift; cast off into the flotsam and jetsam of the military machine. Ever since his Platoon had been separated in Paslek, his sole focus had been on reaching Gdansk and rejoining the Company.

"When is the next ship sailing for Germany, sir?"

The Colonel smiled wryly. "That depends on the Russians," he said. He tapped a satellite image on the back wall. "We expect a major attack from the enemy tomorrow. They're massing their forces to the south and to the east of the city and concentrating their artillery. We plan on evacuating Gdansk tomorrow night. The Brits and the French have a fleet of merchant ships and small commercial craft hidden along the Baltic coast, some as far west as Stralsund in Germany," he touched the photo image. "They're dispersed in small coves and ports to prevent the Russians from discovering what we're planning and bombing the living crap out of them."

McLane listened in silence as the Colonel gave a broad outline of the Allied evacuation plan. The Colonel was making the proposed exodus of a hundred thousand defeated soldiers sound like a brilliant Allied plot; a cunning *ruse de guerre* that would outfox the enemy – instead of the biggest Allied military disaster since the Second World War.

"What am I to do, sir?" McLane let his bitterness edge his voice.

The Colonel made an awkward face and shuffled some papers on his desk like a public servant at an unemployment office. "I'm attaching you to General Donkin's Headquarters."

"General Donkin?"

"He's the American Commander in the city, son."

"You want me to run messages, sir?" McLane's tone turned sour.

"Yes, god-damnit!" the Colonel snapped forward. "I expect you to do whatever the hell the General tells you to do."

"I'd rather fight," McLane persisted stubbornly. "I'm not a pencil-pusher." The Colonel narrowed his eyes, aware that McLane's comment was a thinly-veiled slight on his own administrative role. His expression turned malevolent. The entire city was brimming with bitter, sullen and humiliated soldiers. This Lieutenant from the Mountaineers was just one more arrogant impertinent asshole who felt nothing but contempt for the essential role of Army administration. It was, the Colonel believed, a symptom of the situation. Beaten soldiers were never humble – and these soldiers had been badly beaten at Warsaw. The retreat had frayed tempers and turned disciplined men into a snapping seething mob. Half the troops milling in the city looked like beggars; dressed in rags, unshaven and unkempt.

"The Army doesn't care what you want, Lieutenant. The Army tells you where you are needed, and you obey your orders. Our troops are defending the eastern outskirts of Gdansk. The Brits, Canadians and Poles are protecting the southern flank. General Donkin is setting his defenses along the Oplyw Motlawy moat," the Colonel mangled the pronunciation. "The moat dates back to the seventeenth century and flows along the southern and eastern sides of Gdansk's Old City in a semi-circle." On the wall photograph McLane saw a distinct jagged pattern of blue lines that resembled the zig-zag of an infantry trench.

"The General's HQ is under the Most Siennicki Bridge," the Colonel signed a form on his desk with a dismissive flourish, signaling the end of the meeting. "Report to him in the morning."

*

McLane slept badly and awoke to the thunder of Russian artillery fire.

He lay in the darkness on a hard wooden floor and listened to the dreadful drumming of the explosions that shook the ground and lit the pre-dawn sky with its flickering fury. Nearby Scully and Gardiner stirred, as did many of the others scattered across the floor. There were over a dozen US soldiers in the small room, sleeping rough. One soldier sat up, coughed up a chest full of phlegm, and lit a cigarette. Someone else stirred in the shadows and slowly the room came alert.

The air was stale. A haze of blue smoke hung below the ceiling. Someone opened a window and a chill breeze carried the sound of the enemy guns clearly.

McLane arrived beneath the Most Siennicki Bridge at dawn with Scully and Gardiner in tow. General Donkin's command post was a deserted two-story concrete building with a red-tiled roof that stood at the junction of the Martwa Wisla River and the mouth of the Oplyw Motlawy moat. The premises had been some kind of rowing or sailing club, McLane guessed. There were fiberglass kayaks in a row at the side of the road and a jetty for launching small craft. The parking lot beside the building was filled with an array of military four-wheel drives and Humvees. Inside, the headquarters was in a state of pandemonium. A dozen tables were arranged along the outer walls packed with radio equipment, cords, headphones and harassed operators. In the center of the floor stood a large map of the city pinned to a wheeled whiteboard stand. The stand was surrounded by a knot of uniformed officers, their faces grave. In the middle of the scrum, and reaching a good six inches taller than everyone else in the room, General Willard Donkin was in a thunderous mood.

He was a handsome man with a shock of silver hair and a trim, fit physique. He had a reputation as a no-nonsense straight-talker who did not suffer fools lightly.

An aide leaned close to the General and whispered news in his ear. Donkin's face seemed to suffuse with irritation. Without another word he turned on his heel and stormed across the room to snatch a phone.

"What do we do?" Scully asked from the threshold of the door.

"Wait outside," McLane said. "I'll find out."

He went to the phalanx of radio operators against the far wall, spoke briefly to a uniformed woman, then turned and searched the periphery of the room. He found who he was seeking and strode through the press of bodies.

"Captain Crissman?"

The officer turned, surprised to hear his name called. He was a broad-shouldered, serious-faced man with a pale jagged scar on his chin. "Who wants me?"

"I'm Lieutenant McLane," McLane introduced himself. "I've been sent by Colonel Travis…"

"To do what?"

"Whatever needs doing, sir."

The Captain nodded and drew McLane to a quiet corner of the room. "Look, our communications are a god-damned shambles. Despite all the radio gear you can see, we're struggling to stay connected to our forward units because of Russian electronic counter-measures. They've got everything jammed tighter than a rush hour traffic snarl. So most likely you'll be running messages to the battlefront. Understand?"

McLane nodded.

"But until the Russians decide how they're going to fight this battle there isn't a lot anyone can do. We're waiting, and that's what you'll have to do. There's coffee in a room upstairs. Help yourself, but until the shit hits the fan the best thing you can do is stay out of the way. I'll holler when we need you."

McLane stepped back out into the morning gloom with coffee for Scully and Gardiner. A stray cat lay curled up by the steps of the building and Scully was petting the animal absently.

"Our orders are to hurry up and wait," McLane said.

Scully turned and stared east. The smoke from the enemy's artillery bombardment lay like a dirty haze across the horizon, muting the sunrise. The guns were still firing, pounding the American forward positions, and every few minutes the crack of an artillery round would sound louder that the others, carried downwind by the gusting breeze. McLane sniffed the air. He could smell rain. He crossed to the jetty and stood looking north, through the bomb-ruined streets of Gdansk towards the Baltic Sea. He could see nothing of the sea from where he stood, but he could smell the salt water. Tonight, he would be on a ship bound for Germany.

But first the cobbled-together wreckage of an Allied Army had to somehow survive one more day of killing and chaos.

*

At 7:30 a.m. the Russian guns that had hammered the sky since before dawn suddenly ceased firing. An eerie, ominous pall fell over Gdansk. Smoke from the unending barrage drifted over the heart of the city.

McLane felt a shiver of foreboding run down his spine. The heavy clouds parted and the sun filtered through, threatening to turn the day humid.

"Changing their fire plan?" Private Gardiner looked to McLane for some explanation.

McLane shrugged. "Or preparing to attack."

Russian military doctrine invariably demanded any significant attack be preceded by an intense artillery bombardment. Traditionally, Russia's mobile infantry and armored forces supported the artillery, rather than the reverse. Russia's massed artillery was designed to destroy enemy formations only once their mobile operational ground forces had fixed the enemy to a position. With the Allies pinned to their defensive perimeter across Gdansk's outskirts they became prime targets for massed artillery and rocket fire. But now, after several hours of unending bombardment, Russian Command sensed the task completed. The massed batteries of heavy guns fell silent and soon the tanks would pour forward to crush what remained of the Allied army's resistance and drive the hapless survivors into the sea.

But the anticipated attack did not come.

The Russians, perhaps confident that the Allied troops defending the ruins were on the verge of breaking, seemed in no hurry to send their armored columns forward. Instead a swarm of Russian aircraft appeared from the east, flying low over the coastline. They were Su-25 'Frogfoot' ground attack jets, escorted by MiG-29 'Fulcrum' fighters. Flying top cover, the MiGs banked north to run interference against Polish F-16s on ready alert and a squadron of British Eurofighter Typhoons that were flying combat patrols over the Baltic.

The sky above Gdansk boomed and cracked as the fighters engaged at high altitude. From the ground the savage dogfighting was obscured by low cloud, so that the men in the city could only crane their necks and peer fretfully aloft.

Free to do their deadly work, the first wave of Su-25s swooped low across the city, bombing and strafing the docks and jetties along the Martwa Wisla River and the Kanal Kaszubski. Warehouse buildings along the waterfront were torn apart, bridges destroyed and four small commercial freighters sunk. The air filled with the snarl of 30mm autocannon rounds and the thundering explosions of FAB-500 high-explosive bombs. Two Su-25s were shot down over the waterfront by FIM-92 Stinger MANPADS. The first Russian aircraft was struck as it banked and climbed. The Stinger blew the tail off the enemy jet and it went twisting towards the ocean trailing smoke and fire. The second 'Frogfoot' was destroyed as it swooped down to attack a Dutch freighter in the Kanal Kaszubski. The Stinger streaked across the sky on a tail of white wavering smoke and clipped the wing of the Su-25, sending it spiraling into a bomb-ravaged hotel on Robotnicza Street.

The second wave of Su-25s swept in from the south and hooked east, first attacking British and Canadian armored positions around the outskirt villages of Kowale and Borkowo before swooping over Olszynka where American Abrams tanks were dug in. Their egress from the city was northeast, over the Most Wantowy Bridge which collapsed into the river from multiple Kh-29L laser guided missile impacts.

In their wake, the 'Frogfoots' left a trail of smoke and fire and destruction. Eight British Warrior AFVs were turned to burning hulks, more than three dozen Canadian and British infantry were killed, and four American Strykers had been disintegrated into mangled metal shrapnel.

But still the Russian tanks did not attack.

McLane glanced at his watch. It was past 11:00 a.m. A handful of high-ranking officers stepped out of the headquarters building smoking cigarettes. The wind was dying. Cloud banks still hung low across the sky but here and there patches of sunlight broke through the veil. The officers all turned east and stared at the sullen sky. The minutes passed. None of the officers spoke. The sense of tense trepidation was almost palpable. The sounds of jet fighters in the sky overhead faded until an eerie stillness hung on the air.

Then a Russian gun fired.

The sudden sound rumbled against the low cloud and echoed across the sky. But it had not come from the east as anticipated in the aftermath of the morning's artillery bombardment.

It had come from the south.

Sixty seconds later a second Russian gun fired, and then a third. Captain Crissman came through the front door of the building. He saw McLane and hurried to him.

"It looks like it's started," the Intelligence officer flustered. "Russian tanks are apparently advancing through a little place called Borkowo to the south. We're getting nothing but interference on comms so the General wants eyes and ears. Take a Humvee south, find out what the hell is going on, and how the Brits, Canadians and Poles are holding up. Report back as soon as you can."

*

McLane got onto a highway leading out of the city, driving quickly. The roads were deserted. He found a turnoff to the right that ran through a patch of wooded farmland and then doglegged towards Borkowo. The ground rose the further southwards he travelled, and the sky grew darker behind a billowing front of black smoke. He pulled the Humvee over to the side of the road when he reached the crest of a gentle ridge and snatched for a pair of binoculars. A small roadside signpost read 'Borkowo 2 klm'.

The village was set on level semi-rural land, hemmed between two great grey ribbons of highway.

The British were responsible for this sector of the line; McLane could see several Challenger 2 tanks and field artillery pieces dug in behind earthen emplacements. Although he could not see any infantry, he assumed the British were well dug in on the outskirts of the village and within the bombed ruins.

He swung the binoculars further south, then and gaped in utter disbelief. He had never seen so many Russian tanks; they were advancing in columns between small settlements on the southern skyline and then spreading out into ragged lines once they reached open farmland. On the flanks were swarms of BMP armored personnel carriers – some advancing along the easternmost length of highway and others surging forward across uneven terrain far to the west.

"The Brits will never stop them," even Corporal Scully was overwhelmed and awed by the sight.

The sound of the Russian advance carried clear to where McLane stood; a cacophony of roaring engines as the enemy surged forward along a three mile wide front. Behind the tanks and APCs were support vehicles and transport trucks packed with infantry, and in the air, low and still far in the distance, hung the menace of swarming Russian helicopters.

"They're not interested in finesse," McLane guessed. "They're just going to hammer their way through like a battering ram."

As if in confirmation, the leading line of enemy T-90s popped off smoke canisters to conceal their advance and then accelerated, angling west through fields of tall grass to smash their way through the southern perimeter of the village. A T-90's main gun fired and then a second tank followed – though McLane had no idea what the enemy gunners were aiming at. He saw the twin muzzle flashes and a second later a ruined building in the heart of Borkowo blew apart. Smoke and flames leaped from the destroyed building, adding to the chaos of the battlefield. A moment later the echo of the gunfire slammed across the sky.

McLane guessed the two tank rounds had served as some kind of signal, for suddenly the Russian BMPs on the western flank of the advance turned east and swept across open ground towards the beleaguered village. The armored troop carriers braked to a halt in long grass and infantry spilled out through the rear doors. The troops went forward in a swarm towards the outskirts of Borkowo in order to clear the way for the tanks as they surged closer.

The Russian infantry advanced in a loose skirmish of men, firing as they moved. They reached a stand of trees and from there began to pour concentrated fire into the closest buildings. A handful of British infantry occupying a farm house scrambled back into the main street of the village, leaving several enemy soldiers dead in the grass before they withdrew. The Russians advanced and occupied the farm's buildings then surged forward again under heavy machine gun cover.

The infantry battle in the streets of Borkowo became obscured behind a wall of smoke and the 'crump!' of Russian mortar explosions. The sound of automatic weapons fire rose to a savage snarl.

"I want to take a closer look," McLane said.

Scully drove. She followed the road further south and parked between a complex of fenced-in condominiums and a dense grove of trees. She left the Humvee's engine running. McLane snatched the binoculars to his eyes and peered through the scrims of smoke. Several of the village's buildings were burning and the streets were a haze of dust and flashing, furious noise. The Russians were in the main street of Borkowo now, but meeting fierce resistance from the stubborn British. A Russian mortar team had set up in the captured farm house and was lobbing high-explosive rounds into a block of school buildings.

The British infantry were defending solid brick walls, concealed behind rubble, or fighting from within carefully prepared defenses. They held the determined Russian advance and pushed the enemy back. Dozens of Russians lay dead in the aftermath of the first assault.

The defeated Russians withdrew, but there were more enemy massing in the grove of trees. They came forward with a blood-curdling cheer in their throats, renewing the assault and swarming back through the outskirts so that to McLane it seemed like the ebb and flow of a human tide, washing around buildings that were ringed with smoke.

The British fired and the Russians ran headlong into the incessant fury of their guns. The Russians were unrelenting. Several BMPs nosed their way closer to the village and lent their heavy machine gun support to the enemy infantry. For a few tense minutes it seemed that the additional Russian firepower might turn the momentum of the battle, but then a flurry of flaming white darts plucked at the smoke and streaked across the sky. Three MBPs erupted in fireballs – blown to shrapnel by MBT LAW (NLAW) shoulder-fired disposable anti-tank missiles.

The Russian APCs disengaged and withdrew behind the grove of woods and the Russian infantry were left to fend for themselves. The attack became bogged down. The Russians clung to the southern fringe of the village but could not press on in the face of ferocious British resistance. The firefight continued beneath the pall of smoke as the Russian officers urged their men on.

A fresh Company of Russian infantry tried to reorientate the point of the attack by skirting the western highway and assaulting the village through an area of open farm fields. They dashed forward behind the veil of smoke and reached the back yard fences of a row of houses. The British fired through the fence and from the windows of the homes, but it seemed that the Russians would overwhelm them through sheer weight of numbers. Some Russians reached the fence and lobbed grenades into the back yards where the British were concealed. Other brave men tried to scramble over the wooden pickets but they were plucked back by British guns.

Then a salvo of British mortars opened fire on the milling Russians. The shells rained down on the fence line, striking with murderous precision, cracking apart into balls of flame and swathes of shrapnel. The earth around the Russians heaved and the dust and smoke shrouded them so that to McLane they were temporarily obscured from sight. When the haze began to clear, dozens of Russians lay dead or maimed.

The attack faltered. Some enemy soldiers began to creep backwards. Men stooped to drag injured comrades away from the fighting and others went with them. The British fire from the surrounding buildings seemed to intensify and then a second salvo of British mortar shells plunged down from the clouds, scything through the enemy who were caught in the open.

The surviving Russians retreated. Bloodied and broken they fell back to the highway where their APCs were parked, dragging their wounded with them and hounded by desultory British fire.

"That was nicely done," Corporal Scully had watched the Russian flank attack and acknowledged the skill of the British mortar crews who had turned the tide of the skirmish.

McLane grunted agreement. He still had the binoculars pressed to his eyes and he swung them now back to the heart of the village where the British were still holding. McLane understood that until the British were driven from the village, the enemy advance remained stalled. The Russian tanks could not push through the streets of Borkowo for to do so would be to run a gauntlet of anti-tank missiles.

"They're holding well," McLane said with professional admiration. "The Brits certainly know how to defend a difficult position." He kept his attention on the village, judging the state of the firefight by the sounds and the smoke until Private Gardiner suddenly plucked at his elbow and pointed.

In a fit of frustration and impatience, the Russian commander of tanks had decided to bypass the village entirely by funneling his T-90's through a narrow channel of farmland between the eastern edge of the village and the broad ribbon of highway where his APCs were advancing to protect his eastern flank.

The first line of MBTs compressed into a ragged column behind a huge cloud of dust. McLane watched on, grimly fascinated. The Russian tankers were well drilled and pushed forward quickly.

Then British Challenger 2s opened fire, and the steel tip of the Russian spearhead ran into a wall of fierce resistance.

The Challengers were dug in deep with their backs to a palisade of trees. There was no fallback line; no alternate position. The tankies each knew that there could be no retreat. The British guns opened fire at a range of just a thousand yards and tore bloody holes in the advancing Russian formation. Three T-90s stopped dead in the field, engulfed in billows of black smoke, their tracks smashed rendering them disabled. Two more Russian tanks lurched out of the formation trailing grey smoke.

Still the Russians pushed forward, closing the range quickly. Some tanks tried to push further east and ran through the column of BMPs advancing along the highway, but they were met by Canadian infantry defending that section of the line. The Canadians were equipped with Carl-Gustaf recoilless rifles and American-made BGM-71 TOW anti-tank missiles. They fired from trenches and sandbagged emplacements and the highway became a slaughterhouse of smoke and flames. A handful of BMPs erupted in fireballs and went careening off the highway out of control. Others simply disappeared behind a leaping wall of smoke. Twisted chunks of scorched-black metal lay strewn across the tarmac for hundreds of yards. The road became a junkyard, littered with metal and the crumpled, charred bodies of incinerated Russian infantry. Into this chaos surged the T-90s that sought to outflank the British Challengers. One Russian MBT had its turret cleaved off by the hammer blow of a TOW anti-tank missile. Another T-90 was struck broadside. The missile smashed three of the tank's roadwheels. The Russian tank veered off the highway and plunged out of control down the embankment.

The sickly-sweet smell of burning flesh mingled with the stench of diesel and drifted over the battlefield. The sounds of gunfire and explosions were replaced with the screams of the dying and maimed.

McLane lowered the binoculars and took one long last look at the smoke-filled battlefield. "I've seen enough," he said. The

British were clinging on grimly and for now the southern outskirts of Gdansk were safe. "Take me back to HQ."

Chapter 11:

In the streets of Gdansk's harbor district, the medics were struggling to clear away the dead and dying. While McLane had been to the south of the city, the Russians had resumed their artillery barrage, bringing up a Battalion of eighteen BM-21 'Grad' truck-mounted multiple rocket launchers. The vehicles were parked eight miles east of the city.

As the Humvee turned off the highway and slowed through the inner-city streets on its way back to General Donkin's headquarters, the sky overhead suddenly filled with a hail of comet-like fiery streaks.

A thundering volley of over seven hundred rockets plunged down across the city, the sound of them through the air a ferocious shriek of doom. They exploded indiscriminately across several city blocks, causing catastrophic mayhem and chaos. Buildings caught on fire. Others collapsed, killing rescue crews on the streets below. Critical harbor infrastructure blew apart and a small freighter in a repair dock was damaged. McLane heard the evil whistle of the incoming rockets and knew there was not enough time to seek cover. Scully stopped the Humvee by the side of the road and all three Americans simply ducked down, covered their heads and prayed.

The Humvee shook as the stampede of Russian rockets plunged down out of the sky. None landed close to the Humvee, but the trail of their destructive path was clear to see from the windshield of the vehicle. Each rocket exploded in a vast plume of sheeted flames that rose hundreds of feet into the sky. Rubble and debris fell like rain and clouds of black smoke rolled through the narrow streets thick as morning fog.

Scully stabbed her foot on the gas pedal and the Humvee leaped forward, swerving around falling wreckage that continued to tumble from the sky. When they reached the General's headquarters, they found the staff in a state of pandemonium and panic.

McLane leaped from the Humvee and pushed his way through a crowd of milling anxious junior officers. He found Captain Crissman by the bank of radios. Most of the stations were deserted, the comms gear left unattended. Crissman was talking urgently into a microphone. When he saw McLane striding across the room, he abruptly broke the connection and snatched off the headset.

"The British?"

"They're holding," McLane confirmed. The words hung in the stuffy smoke-hazed air of the room.

"Thank God," Crissman allowed himself a brief moment of relief. "Tell me what you saw."

McLane strode to the map on the whiteboard stand and traced a filthy finger across the village of Borkowo. "The Russians tried to take the village with a series of infantry attacks, but the British held them off. Then the Russians pushed their tanks forward, trying to bypass the village and break through our lines. Challengers stopped the attack and then Canadian infantry fired on a column of enemy APCs, blocking the highway."

"You saw all this?"

"Yes."

Crissman looked up into McLane's eyes. "Are you sure the Brits can continue to hold?"

"They're having a hard time of it," McLane admitted. "But their lines were solid and they know their trade. Yes. They can hold – at least until dark."

"That might buy us the time we need."

"Need for what?" McLane frowned.

"To evacuate," the Intelligence officer said.

"Now? Already? I was told the rescue ships weren't arriving until nightfall."

Crissman smiled thinly, but there was no amusement in his expression. "The Russians attacked from the east thirty minutes ago under artillery and rocket fire. They broke straight through our lines. Our Abrams formed the first defensive perimeter; they were well dug in and under camouflage netting. The Russians took heavy losses but rolled right over them. Our tanks pulled back to the railway lines at Olszynka," Crissman pointed to the east of the city where a series of train tracks ran past an outlying residential district, "and we're holding them there at the moment – but not for long. NATO command has moved up the timeline. It's put an emergency call out to the flotilla to arrive asap. The ships should start appearing on the horizon in a couple of hours. We have to try for a daylight evacuation."

McLane studied the map closely. The nearest Russian tanks were less than three kilometers away. Suddenly he understood the panic that had infected General Donkin's headquarters staff.

"What about our infantry?"

Crissman looked pained. "The last time we had radio contact they were holding the houses west of the railway lines but they were under attack from Russian motorized rifle units and APCs. They were running low on Javelins. God knows if they're still alive…"

"What's being done to re-supply them?"

Captain Crissman looked darkly bemused. "We can't get to them."

"Let me try," McLane volunteered impulsively. He understood the significance of the situation. The American Abrams MBTs needed the support of infantry, and the one thing the Russian tanks would fear in an urban street-fight would be well-trained enemy armed with anti-tank weapons. If the American troops on the ground were still alive, and if they could be re-supplied with Javelins quickly, there was still a chance the Allied line on the eastern outskirts of the city could hold.

Crissman shook his head. "The General has ordered the headquarters evacuated. We're pulling out and moving to the harbor." As if to confirm the urgency of the order a series of ragged explosions sounded to the east. Somewhere, not too far away, tanks were engaging. The windows in the building rattled against their casements. The sound faded and was replaced by rising panicked voices. People began moving out through the building's doors to where a fleet of Humvees and four-wheel drives were waiting to spirit them away. A dozen uniformed soldiers swarmed into the building to load the comms gear.

"Let me try reaching our infantry," McLane pinned Crissman with the intensity of his voice. "They deserve a fighting chance to defend their position."

Crissman hesitated. He too understood the importance of Olszynka. If the infantry there were overrun, then the Russians would punch through the gap and drive unchallenged into the heart of the city. The American tanks would be isolated and surrounded, and the British, Canadians, and Poles fighting to the south would be encircled and destroyed. "Okay."

McLane bounded out through the door suddenly filled with purpose, followed by the Captain. "There is a weapons depot two blocks south of here," Crissman said. "I'll radio ahead and tell them to expect you."

McLane nodded. He shouted for Scully and Gardiner then clambered into the Humvee. He yelled for Scully to climb behind the wheel. A group of junior officers, alerted by McLane's shouting had gathered in the parking lot in a state of anxious alarm. Crissman waved them aside. "When you hear air-raid sirens, it's the signal to get to the harbor. Once the sirens start, it's the beginning of the end, so move your ass."

McLane nodded. Scully crushed the gas pedal under her foot and the Humvee roared out of the parking lot. McLane threw Captain Crissman an impulsive salute, and then went to find a fight.

*

The Russian armored attack across the eastern districts of Gdansk had come suddenly and unexpectedly. In the eerie lull between artillery bombardments, the T-90s assembled into ranks behind the lingering smoke that drifted across the city's outskirts and then, without fanfare or being announced by another fearful artillery barrage, the steel beasts swarmed out of the mist and swept across the vast patchwork of farm fields.

The American Abrams, hull down in deep trenches, had time for just a couple of hurried shots before they were forced to fall back to their alternate positions along the Olszynka rail line. The Russians swept through the outlying districts and then slammed into the American infantry defending the western edge of the railway tracks. The homes throughout the Olszynka district were neatly spaced and well-tended on quarter-acre blocks. The Russians reached the railway lines and a close-quarters battle between the two tank forces erupted. The Americans were on the backfoot and vastly outnumbered. The grid of suburban streets became a deadly maze. One Abrams under heavy fire reversed around a blind corner and was destroyed by a T-90 with a rear shot from close range. Another cornered Abrams backed itself into the rubble of a destroyed building and was set upon by three T-90s. One of the Russian tanks took a disabling hit to its roadwheels before the Abrams was destroyed by two close-range turret hits.

Into the madness poured Russian infantry, sped to the battlefront aboard BMP-2 armored personnel carriers. They reached the Olszynka railway lines and dismounted in the face of fierce American infantry fire. The Americans were barricaded in the houses facing the railway tracks and as the Russian motorized infantry units spilled from their vehicles, a whip-lash of Javelin missiles raced across the sky. Four of the Russian BMPs exploded in quick succession, tearing the steel vehicles into flying steel fragments. Dozens of Russians fell in the first few murderous minutes of the battle. More enemy APCs appeared through the smoke and slowly, gradually, the Americans were forced back as the battle evolved into a door-to-door street fight.

The gutters ran with blood. Bodies became piled up atop each other as the overwhelmed Americans made the Russians pay a cruel price for every inch of ground gained. A two-man Javelin team barricaded in the top floor of a house on Miodowa Street saw a T-90 turn the corner and come rumbling towards them. The Russian tank roared past, kicking up a trail of dust as it raced towards the far end of the road to blindside a reversing Abrams. The Javelin missile struck the rear of the T-90 with such savage force that for an instant the enemy tank was rocked on its tracks as the missile detonated. The tank erupted in flames and oily black smoke, and burned like an inferno. Russian infantry who witnessed the Javelin attack opened fire on the house where the Americans were concealed, killing the two-man team and partially demolishing the house with grenades.

More Russians poured into the streets, a seemingly endless tide of enemy soldiers and APCs. The sounds of gunfire became ceaseless. The Americans continued to fall back, dragging their wounded with them. A squad of Russians advancing ahead of their APC were ambushed by American fire from both sides of a street and slaughtered to a man. The gunner aboard the trailing BMP fired his autocannon into the nearby buildings in retribution until a Javelin missile streaked across the smoke-stained sky and tore the vehicle to pieces in a whoosh of flames and a thunderclap of noise. More Russians converged on the street, pining the Americans to their precarious position. The leading Russians charged to reach the buildings and were cut down. Wounded men screamed in pain and the blacktop became drenched in Russian blood. As the front men fell, those behind leaped over their dying comrades, firing wildly into the smoke and confusion. Then a T-90 rounded the corner and opened fire, blowing one building, and then the other, to rubble. The handful of defiant Americans were killed in the blasts and the blood-drenched street feel eerily silent beneath a billowing cloud of dust.

McLane arrived on the western outskirts of Olszynka district, into the blood and the slaughter. Scully drove the Humvee up onto a sidewalk and behind the cover of a house. McLane flung himself from the vehicle and narrowed his eyes, his instincts attuned to the sounds of the raging battle. Most of the gunfire and explosions were coming from somewhere due east, but to the south and the north the sky was filled with columns of billowing smoke.

"Come on!"

They went east, clinging to the sidewalks, moving from house to house like thieves. The sound of gunfire ebbed and flowed, then rose to a savage crescendo as they passed one intersection after another. Bodies lay sprawled on the blacktop. Some lay motionless, others groaned softly. One Russian infantryman lay in the gutter in a puddle of blood and vomit. He had been shot twice in the torso. Flies crawled across the dead man's open staring eyes and laid their eggs in the gaping hole of his open mouth.

Closer to the sounds of fighting they passed a burning Russian BMP-2. The vehicle was a blackened mangled wreck and around the ruins were several charred bodies, hideously writhed and disfigured. The stench of burning flesh and oil was choking. It caught in the back of McLane's throat and he gagged. Nearby they found the first of the Americans. There were three dead men in the rubble of a ruined house. One soldier had been shot in the head from close range, the damage so gruesome that his features were unrecognizable. The other two had been torn to shreds by an exploding grenade. All three corpses lay in a pool of sticky spreading blood, their remains powdered grey by drifting dust.

"Leave them," McLane lowered his voice to a whisper. "There's nothing we can do."

Ahead of him the road intersected with a side street. McLane crept to the corner, crouched low, his guts sour with fear and tension. On the far side of the blacktop, about a hundred yards away, he could see a squad of Russian infantry moving along a shadowed laneway, their weapons held at the ready, their eyes on the windows of the buildings as they passed. When they reached the end of the lane and emerged into the gloomy daylight, they were mercilessly cut down by a blast of automatic weapons fire that came from a house fifty yards to McLane's right.

Four of the Russians were killed outright in the savage fusillade. Three more went down screaming in pain. One soldier dropped to his knees clawing at his eyes, his face a mask of blood. The two surviving Russians fired wildly and retreated into the shadows of the alley.

"Follow me!" McLane hissed.

They went right, across a backyard fence, through a plot of tomatoes and beans, then over another fence. Rifle fire and the roaring boom of explosions echoed across the sky. Thick smoke washed around McLane in waves so that he groped forward like a blind man. "Americans!" he raised his voice. "Americans!"

Suddenly a huge hand loomed out of the choking haze. It seized McLane's shoulder, pulling him roughly off balance. A dark shape thrust the barrel of an M4 in his face. Other dark figures surrounded Scully and Gardiner.

"Who the fuck are you?" the voice was tight and edged with hair-trigger tension.

"Lieutenant Simon McLane," he identified himself. "We've been sent from HQ with Javelins."

*

The infantry Captain defending the block of buildings had no time for pleasantries for on the far side of the street Russian infantry were massing behind half a dozen BMPs and preparing to launch yet another assault.

"Orders?"

"None," McLane told the Captain. "I just brought Javelins."

McLane sent Scully and Gardiner back to fetch the Humvee and crept to a ground floor window to stare out across the street. The interior walls of the building were riddled with bullet holes, the windows smashed. The floor was strewn with broken furniture, shards of glass and dust. A wounded rifleman lay slumped in the far corner, his head swathed in bloodied bandages, and an IV drip hooked up to his arm.

A Russian mortar shell crashed into the roof of the house next door, showering the street with roof tiles. McLane surveyed the damage all around him and grimaced. "Can you hold out?"

The Captain looked bleak. His face was cut above his eyebrow and his cheeks streaked with dirt. "Fuck knows," he said. "We lost the last of the Abrams about thirty minutes ago. If we don't get reinforced…" he left the rest of the dire prophecy unsaid.

There were infantrymen spread throughout the building, manning every window and every crumbled piece of wall. The Company was stretched across the length of the entire block, spread thin and worn down by mortar fire and wave after wave of Russian attacks.

A series of shrill whistles sounded and a moment later the blacktop filled with smoke grenades. Into the swirling haze, the Russians poured. Some streamed out of the buildings on the far side of the street. Others appeared from out of BMPs that converged on the nearby intersection.

"Here they come again!" the infantry Captain cried the warning.

The Americans opened fire from close range. Bullets plucked at the smoke as the street filled with dark silhouetted shapes. Tongues of flickering flame leaped from the windows and the Russians began to fall. Twenty enemy soldiers went down in the first furious seconds. The Russians returned fire as they charged and the BMPs added their brutal autocannons to the fusillade. One American soldier took the impact of a 30mm round full in the chest and his body disintegrated in a gruesome splatter of flesh and bones. Another man was shot twice in the arm and fell to the ground sobbing in excruciating pain.

"Fire!" the infantry Captain's voice became harsh and desperate. The Americans were on the verge of being overwhelmed. The Russians reached the sidewalk and sought the cover of fences and shrubs. "Kill them!"

The smoke-filled road ahead of McLane was crammed with Russians. They dashed towards a low fence that enclosed a front yard garden. One enemy soldier fired and then threw a smoke grenade. McLane shot him in the chest and saw the impact of the bullet slam the soldier onto the ground. He fired again, hitting the man in the thigh, then changed aim and fired at a Russian Sergeant who was shouting at the others around him, rallying them, driving them forward. McLane missed the Sergeant. The bullet took one of the running men behind the big Russian full in the face. His head snapped back and he fell.

"Kill the bastards!"

It turned into a savage gutter fight. McLane stepped over the body of a dead American medic and leaned around a doorway to fire at a knot of enemy soldiers that had reached the cover of a burned-out car. Dead Russians were scattered across the road. Some lay in the gutters. Some were piled up on the sidewalk. Another rifleman joined McLane in the doorway. His left hand was swathed in bloody bandages and his face and uniform were spattered with fresh gore. Together they drove the Russians back with a withering burst of fire. A snarling Russian hefting a light machine gun turned and braced the weapon against his hip, then sprayed the doorway with counterfire. McLane ducked behind a brick wall but the rifleman at his side reacted an instant too late. Two bullets struck him in the neck. He was dead before his body hit the ground.

Then the sound of a sudden explosion to their rear startled the Americans and filled them with ice-cold dread. McLane turned, M4 raised and his eyes wide with shock, to see the Humvee burst into sight. Scully had crashed across back yards and through neighborhood fences to deliver their cargo of Javelins, rather than risk the roads that were swarming with enemy tanks and troop carriers.

The spare missiles reached the anti-tank teams and two Russian BMP-2s erupted in flames in quick succession – but it was too little, too late.

The Russians were ferocious. A snarling officer with yellow teeth and bleeding lips lead a squad of charging enemy soldiers into a house further along the street. The *'crump!'* of grenades shook the building and the front room erupted in flames. A roar of gunfire drowned out sudden screams and shouts, and then the enemy officer emerged onto the sidewalk, stepping over the twitching bodies of slaughtered Americans. He gave a great primal roar of triumph, his uniform drenched in blood.

With their line overwhelmed and the enemy in their midst, the American Captain realized the fight was over, but he stubbornly refused to accept defeat. He cursed in bitter despair and raised his voice to an urgent shout.

"Stand and fight! Stand and fight!"

It was suicidal. The Russians were pouring fresh infantry through the breach in the line, and beginning to enfilade the remaining Americans from the flanks. In minutes the Americans would be completely surrounded and slaughtered. There was only one chance that any of them might survive.

"Run!" It was McLane's voice. Some of the nearby infantrymen began to back away from the walls and windows they defended, giving ground but fighting on grimly. Others turned, torn with confusion.

"Keep fighting!" the infantry Captain yelped at the men around him.

"Break and run!"

A Russian soldier fired into the chaos of smoke and killed the American Captain. His cries of suicidal defiance strangled in his throat.

"Run! Get to the harbor!"

It became a deadly race. If the Americans could disengage and reach the western outskirts of the district, they could get across the moat and make their way to the harbor, but if the Russians pressed home their advantage and swamped the district with APCs and fresh squads of infantry, the Americans would be cornered and killed.

The Russians pressed home their advantage.

A column of BMP-2s came trundling down a nearby street trailing a huge plume of brown dust in their wake, their steel hulls crammed with soldiers eager to join in the slaughter. The gunners in the vehicle's turrets swung their machine guns on the scattering Americans and cut them down mercilessly.

An American infantryman running for his life turned and saw three Russians pursuing him. He dropped to his knee to fire but was shot several times. He screamed and then fell writhing on the sidewalk. The Russians left him by the side of the road to bleed out and ran past him. Another man was callously run down by the driver of a BMP-2 and crushed beneath the vehicle's grinding steel tracks. The American retreat became a chaotic terror-stricken rout and McLane, Scully and Gardiner were swept up in the carnage.

In a single fateful moment, the battle for Gdansk had ended.

The fight for survival had just begun.

*

McLane, Scully and Gardiner reached the Humvee. Scully threw the vehicle into reverse and crushed her foot on the gas pedal. The Humvee roared backwards through broken fencing and across a garden, churning the lawn. Private Gardiner scrambled up through the vehicle's turret ring and hunched behind the 50cal machine gun. He cranked the handle with his left hand to turn the turret, and as the Humvee continued to lurch wildly in reverse, he opened fire.

"Enemy APC! Enemy APC!" McLane called targets from the passenger seat. "Engage!"

Gardiner swung the heavy machine gun and opened fire. The whip-crack of bullets streaked across the ruins of the street and a hail of empty shell casings sprayed like rain from the breach.

"Last hit was good! Lead it about a half inch more!" McLane shouted.

Gardiner fired again. The Russian BMP-2 disappeared behind a wall of smoke.

"Dismounts! Dismounts!" enemy infantry swarmed from every direction, pouring through the hole in the American line. They were shouting their savage triumph as they fell upon the shattered Americans. The Humvee's 50cal cut a swathe through the Russian infantry and the gutters ran with fresh blood and gore. McLane had a glimpse of an enemy soldier kneeling to fire at the vehicle as it sped away. He ducked his head and felt the heat of the bullet fan his face as it passed an inch wide of his ear. Another Russian aimed and fired. The windshield of the Humvee starred and shattered. McLane fired back with his M4, spraying a wild burst of bullets that churned the air but missed his target.

The Humvee sideswiped a wooden shed. Scully turned the vehicle, churning the lawn to muddy ruins and stabbed her foot on the gas pedal. The vehicle sped west, drawing fire from a BMP-2 as it swerved and veered towards safety. Enemy bullets punched through the Humvee's steel sides, narrowly missing McLane.

Swirls of black choking dust drifted across the road and Scully steered into it, concealing them from the enemy's guns. When the haze cleared, the Humvee had reached the western outskirts of the settlement and was hurtling over a bridge across the Oplyw Motlawy moat. Behind them Olszynka district was a ruin of fiery rubble and smoke and untold death.

The sound of wailing sirens rose in the distance, their mournful, strident warning echoing from all parts of the city. It was the warning that the flotilla of ships intended to carry them to safety was looming on the horizon.

It was the sound of retreat and inglorious defeat.

McLane reloaded his M4 with a fresh magazine and gave Scully a savage look. "Get us to the harbor!"

*

The vast motley collection of Allied rescue ships appeared on the skyline behind a smudge of brown smoke. There were ships and boats of every type – from grimy dust-stained freighters to coastal ferries to commercial fishing trawlers and even sail craft. Over the horizon and in the deep water of the

Baltic a taskforce of six American, British and French destroyers kept watch over the brood, their surface-to-air missiles on standby for action.

In the skies above the fleet circled Polish F-16 Fighting Falcons and German Luftwaffe Eurofighter Typhoons flying combat air patrols over the vulnerable flotilla. The pilots were tense, their eyes cast to the east, searching for the first signs of enemy jets.

Fifteen thousand feet below the circling fighters, the dockyards along the city's harbor front were crammed with gathering mobs of anxious soldiers. They poured across the railway lines and over the footbridge near the Gdansk Stocznia train station, then milled around the towering cranes that stood alongside the Gdansk Shipyard. The massive building's landmark blue gates were wide open and there were more men lining the dockyard's waterfront, their eyes cast nervously towards the eastern sky.

Other men poured across the Na Ostrowiu Bridge and gathered along the jetties and piers around the Basen Ostrowica III marina. Soon the entire Mlyniska quarter was thronged with waiting Allied soldiers, some injured or wounded, some snapping and shoving to force their way closer to the waterfront and thus be amongst the first evacuated to safety.

Scully drove the Humvee as far as the Most Siennicki Bridge before the road towards the waterfront became hopelessly logjammed with a chaos of abandoned vehicles. They ditched the Humvee and raced across the bridge. McLane looked left as he ran; the inner harbor front was crammed with thousands of soldiers.

"Which way?" Scully asked when they reached the northern side of the bridge. To head left would take them along the crowded waterfront. McLane followed a hunch.

"Keep going north towards the coast!"

They ran. The streets on the northern side of the Martwa Wisla were almost deserted. McLane could smell the scent of the ocean and hear the far-off sounds of jet fighters. He ran until his chest ached and the breath sawed painfully across his throat. The sounds of snarling jets grew louder. He searched the sky but saw nothing except black smoke. Gdansk was burning, and the afternoon had been plunged into an eerie twilight.

When they reached the coastline, they burst onto a stretch of sand. McLane sagged, bent over at the waist with his hands on his knees, sucking in deep breaths. To their left stretched a vast container terminal. "Go! Go! Go!"

He could see the nearest vessels of the flotilla. They were still a couple of miles off shore, but closing quickly. The larger ships were sailing towards the mouth of the harbor and for a moment he feared he had made a dreadful mistake. He ran on, watching the ships slowly approach.

The vast platform of the container terminal thrust eight hundred yards into the waters of the Baltic. The western edge of the huge pier was lined with heavy ship-loading cranes. McLane gaped in shock and dismay. There were thousands of Allied soldiers crammed along the length of the terminal; how they had arrived there he had no idea.

He felt a primal rise of panic, but kept running. Off the coast, dozens of trawlers and small sailing craft were peeling away from the main flotilla and sailing towards the outer harbor where McLane and the others anxiously waited. They were at the back of a throng, far from the edge of the jetty. Thousands of soldiers ahead of them were pushing and shoving like a crowd at the gates to a football stadium. Tempers rose and men turned on each other, snarling. The smell of raw fear and panic hung in the air.

From out of nowhere the eastern sky came alive with the roar and snarl of Russian fighter jets. They came in two waves; MiG-29s dueled at high altitude with Allied fighters while deadly Su-25 'Frogfoots' skimmed low over the burning landscape, spitting vengeance.

McLane saw the Su-25s as dark specks against the clouds of billowing smoke and realized in a moment of gut-sickening clarity the mistake he had made. He turned, frantic, and then seized Scully and Gardiner by the arms. "Come on!"

"Where?" Gardiner looked mortified. The nearest trawlers and sailboats were within a kilometer of the great cargo container pier. Rescue was just a few minutes away.

"Back to the beach!" McLane growled. He pushed them, shoved them and they went reluctantly. A handful of other soldiers milling at the back of the horde overhead McLane and ran with them.

The Su-25s came sweeping along the coastline, following the thin yellow ribbon of sand as they prepared to attack. Under their wings were payloads of BETAB-500 SHP bombs. McLane looked up, and saw the evil shaped shadows of the Russian beasts pass overhead with a roar of howling noise.

Six hundred yards east of the container terminal the 'Frogfoots' opened fire with their machine guns, stitching the vast expanse of concrete platform with a hail of burning lead. The Allied soldiers on the pier scattered but there was nowhere to run. Dozens were cut down as the first 'Frogfoots' swept past. Men fell bleeding and screaming. Others were struck and tumbled into the water. A collective cry of panic broke out as the hapless Allied troops scattered for cover.

Behind the first echelon of Frogfoots followed the second wave of Su-25s. As they approached the terminal they climbed slightly, then loosed the bombs hanging beneath their wings.

McLane saw the gruesome horror unfold from the beach. Six BETAA-500 SHP bombs struck the great concrete platform and blew it apart. The piers collapsed, the great deck of concrete heaved up and then disappeared in a vast flash of flames and a great billowing cloud of roiling black smoke. When the haze cleared, the western half of the container terminal had collapsed into the Baltic, taking thousands of Allied soldiers to their death.

Scully gaped, her face ashen with shock. "Oh, Jesus!"

McLane could hear the screaming now; the shrieks of terror and pain.

"Oh, fuck…" Private Gardiner breathed. The water was churned white, parts of the shattered concrete dangling from their crushed piers. The cries of the drowning grew louder. Stacked shipping containers that had been piled three high along the terminal ready for loading slid into the ocean, crushing hundreds. Two huge steel cranes toppled over and plunged down on top of the carnage, burying the drowning masses under thousands of tons of steel.

The Su-25s flew on, wheeling south once they reached the mouth of the harbor and flying low along the river, firing their machine guns and dropping their bombs on the crowded troops that crammed the waterfront. Fresh explosions bloomed along the skyline.

Through the smoke, a flotilla of brave little boats emerged, bobbing on the turbulent waves as they nosed closer to the shore. They split east and west of the wrecked container terminal; the larger boats steering for the long thrusting finger of the Pomost Rudowy coal loading terminal and the smaller craft turning east towards the beach where McLane, Scully, Gardiner and several dozen other soldiers waited.

McLane turned and looked again to the east. The Su-25s were circling the city and returning for another cruel attack along the shoreline. The closest approaching boat was a small ferry, painted yellow and green and stained with soot, sitting low in the water, its sides streaked with orange scars of rust.

"Go!" McLane said impulsively. He threw off his heavy equipment and ran down the beach. Gardiner and Scully followed. McLane reached the waterline just as the ferry turned clumsily broadside and two longboats were lowered into the sea. "Swim for it!" McLane shouted.

The two boats were pushing away from the ferry's hull, oars dipping and rising. McLane lost his footing in the white-water of the shore breakers and went under. Scully grabbed him by the collar and hauled him to the surface. More men sprinted from the beach and plunged into the ocean. The closest Su-25 began firing, strafing the sand with its powerful machine gun. Bullets whipped and slashed through the air.

One French soldier was cut down as the Russian ground attack aircraft streaked by so low that the air shook and quivered with the pressure wave of their passing.

The second echelon of Russian jets appeared out of the haze. McLane waved his arms desperately and one of the longboats turned towards him. Two of the 'Frogfoots' opened fire on the men in the water. Bullets plunged and fizzed past McLane's face, churning the sea to a boiling frenzy. Two other Su-25s strafed the little ferry, punching holes in the stern deck and shattering the glass windows of the wheelhouse but causing no mortal wounds. A freighter steaming a few hundred yards to the west of the ferry took the full brunt of the fusillade and suddenly erupted in a billow of smoke and licking oily flames. She was an old clunker of a ship, battered and scaly under a rust-streaked coat of grey paint. The freighter began to wallow in the water and took on a list to starboard.

McLane waved his arms again. He was chest deep in the water, the waves lapping over his head, his boots weighing him down like anchors. He retched a mouthful of oily salt water and spluttered and gasped for breath.

Finally, the longboat reached McLane. He stretched a weary arm up and clung to the transom. A hand reached down and seized him by the collar, pulling the deadweight of him unceremoniously aboard like a landed fish. Then more hands were reaching for Scully and Gardiner.

"Pull!" a Frenchman at the boat's oars called to his shipmates. More men were dragged aboard until the little boat was so overloaded it had seawater sloshing over its gunwales. It turned then, the oarsmen slapping at the sea as the boat rocked around and nudged its nose towards the ocean.

McLane slumped in the bottom of the boat and stared numbly back at the burning city. The sky over Gdansk was lurid with the orange glow of flames. He felt dazed and overwhelmed. He made eye contact with Private Gardiner and then Corporal Scully.

They had survived.

Epilogue:

Long after darkness fell, and well after the ragged flotilla of ships had sailed beyond the horizon, the glow of Gdansk burning still lit the skyline.

McLane, Scully, and Private Gardiner stood at the ferry's stern rail staring into the blackness, each alone with their memories and nightmares.

The ferry was crammed with soldiers; so dangerously overloaded that it dared not steam at more than a few knots, barely making headway against the current.

Scully watched the water being churned to froth by the ferry's twin screws for a long time and then turned to McLane, pain and grief in her eyes.

"Thousands died today," she said softly. "And Poland has fallen to the Russians."

"Yes," McLane admitted. "We've lost this campaign, but the war isn't over. We'll come back, Scully. One day the Allies will march into Poland again."

"How can you be so sure?" Scully muttered.

"Because we have to. We owe it to men like Sergeant Block and Lieutenant Barnsley from the Royal Tank regiment. We have to be sure their heroism wasn't wasted and wasn't in vain. We owe them, and all the men who died fighting, a debt of honor that only the ultimate liberation of Poland can repay…"

A ship somewhere in the night blew its whistle and the master of the ferry sounded his horn in acknowledgement. It was a low, mournful wail that carried across the still night.

It sounded like a sad lament for the dead.

Facebook: https://www.facebook.com/NickRyanWW3
Website: https://www.worldwar3timeline.com

Author's note:

For the sake of the story, I have deliberately manipulated the geography of a couple of village locations in northern Poland, and altered their features. I've also added a bridge crossing that does not exist. I hope Polish readers familiar with the locations will forgive me the literary license I have taken.

Acknowledgements:

The greatest thrill of writing, for me, is the opportunity to research the subject matter and to work with military, political and historical experts from around the world. I had a lot of help researching this book from the following groups and people. I am forever grateful for their willing enthusiasm and cooperation. Any remaining technical errors are mine.

Richard Cutland:

Richard retired from the British Army as a Warrant Officer after a distinguished 30-year career with the Royal Tank Regiment, predominately serving on Main Battle Tanks such as the Challenger 2. He deployed on numerous Operational Tours, is a veteran of the Gulf War, and has worked with many of the world's Armed Forces. He also spent two years as a Gunnery Instructor teaching new tank commanders and overseas students whilst running live firing ranges in the UK and Germany. Richard has a passion for military history and also taught armored tactics.

Since leaving the British Army Richard has become the Head of Military Relations Europe for the wildly popular PC Game World of Tanks.

Jill Blasy:

Jill has the editorial eye of an eagle! I trust Jill to read every manuscript, picking up typographical errors, missing commas, and for her general 'sense' of the book. Jill has been a great friend and a valuable part of my team for several years.

Jan Wade:

Jan is my Personal Assistant and an indispensable part of my team. She is a thoughtful, thorough, professional and persistent pleasure to work with. Chances are, if you're reading this book, it's due to Jan's engaging marketing and promotional efforts.

The Royal Tank Regiment:

My thanks to the British Army's social media representatives at the Royal Tank Regiment who were kind enough to answer some of my research questions about the Challenger 2 MBT. Their assistance helped to ensure accuracy and provided small, important details that all served to enhance the authenticity of my descriptions.

Dale Simpson:

Dale is a retired Special Forces operator who has been helping me with the military aspects of my writing since I first put pen to paper. He is my first point of contact for military technical advice. Over the years that he has been saving me from stupid mistakes we've become firm friends. The authenticity of the action and combat sequences in this novel are due to Dale's diligence and willing cooperation.

Dale proudly served with the men of the 10th Mountain Division in Logar Provence, Afghanistan, in 2011.

Dion Walker Sr:

Sergeant First Class (Retired) Dion Walker Sr, served 21 proud years in the US Army with deployments during Operation Desert Shield/Storm, Operation Intrinsic Action and Operation Iraqi Freedom. For 17 years he was a tanker in several Armor Battalions and Cavalry Squadrons before spending 4 years as an MGS (Stryker Mobile Gun System) Platoon Sergeant in a Stryker Infantry Company.

Graham Collins:

Graham served with the 1st Royal Tank Regiment in the British Army as a crew commander in a Close Recce Troop which worked with British Armored Battle Groups to locate the enemy, provide reconnaissance screens and provide flank protection. Graham's specialized knowledge of Armored Battle Group tactics and its doctrine were instrumental in helping me to understand the way Allied and Axis armored units operated, especially when writing the book's climactic battle sequences.

Printed in Great Britain
by Amazon